The UNFORGETTABLE Tales of ADELINE BIGSBY

CALEB'S STORY
BOOK 3

ELIZABETH MOWERY

Wild & Free
—PUBLISHING—

Published by Wild & Free Publishing LLC, Tobaccoville, NC 27050

Library of Congress Control Number: 2026912866

ISBN: 979-8-9900151-5-9 (Paperback)

ISBN: 979-8-9900151-4-2 (eBook edition)

Cover Design by Vivien Reis and Adam Mowery

To my amazing Dad, for always being in my corner and cheering me on.

Chapter One

Sunlight streamed through the cabin windows as Adeline Bigsby leaned against the armrest and spread a blanket over her lap. Caleb Wilder sat silently on the opposite couch, staring into the coffee that had gone cold. She smoothed the fabric with tired fingers. She wasn't cold, but its soft weight offered some comfort against the suffocating grief seeping into her bones.

She couldn't believe Jesse was dead. The friend who had become like a brother to her gone in an instant. All because she'd tried to be a hero.

The instant her arrow pierced his back replayed in her mind. Guilt consumed her. Jesse's death was her fault, and no one could convince her otherwise.

Adeline rubbed her pounding forehead, her weary fingers doing little to ease the pain. Everything hurt. Her muscles. Her head. But most of all, her heart. It had shattered in a single, irreversible moment.

The tightness in her chest refused to relent as she watched Caleb, waiting for him to begin his story. He looked so different from when she'd first met him in the Red-Rock Region.

Both of his golden-green eyes were severely bruised, his right one still swollen shut. A faint shadow of stubble lined his sharp jaw, and his shaved head was no longer burdened by dreadlocks that had once hung past his shoulders.

Each time she looked at him, she felt his pain. His face was a map of bruises, each one a painful reminder of what he'd endured with Ralock and his military. They had nearly beaten the life out of him. A split lip and the gap of a missing tooth made the damage stand out even more.

Caleb was the reason she had escaped the Dark Territory. If he hadn't been so persistent in saving her, she would have died beside Jesse. Then again, part of her wondered if that might have been the better option. She already felt like death had struck her.

She didn't know Caleb well, but she was glad he was with her. The cabin had been empty when they'd arrived, offering no clues about where Godfrey and Henry Snow were. For now, she was grateful they weren't home. She wasn't ready to face them. Not yet.

"Are you sure you want to hear my story?" Caleb asked, running a hand over his shaved head.

He had no idea that Adeline had been dying to know all about him since they had met. She'd hated him at first—had almost killed him, in fact—but her curiosity had never faded. She'd always wondered how he'd found this strange world, and what had driven him to hate her friends so much.

"Yeah," she said, her voice hoarse.

Caleb looked her way, and a wave of insecurity rushed in. She'd seen herself in the mirror. Her face was blotchy from crying, her eyes were puffy, and bruises darkened her fair skin, making her look every bit as broken as she felt.

The worst part wasn't her appearance, but that he was seeing her so vulnerable, so weak. There was no hiding it.

Caleb leaned back, his gaze flickering around the cabin as though the walls themselves haunted him. His hands fidgeted with the mug in his lap. Adeline could see the battle in him: the hesitation, the fear, the urge to keep everything locked inside.

She held her breath, bracing herself. Whatever he was about to say, it wouldn't be good.

Finally, he drew a shaky breath. "I found this world when I was fifteen."

His good eye slid shut, and for a moment the sunlight seemed to fade. The silence pressed in, broken only by his quick, ragged breaths as if the past itself had forced its way into the room. Adeline's grip on the blanket tightened. It was like watching him get dragged away before her eyes, pulled back into a place he didn't want to go.

He wasn't with her anymore. He was somewhere else, reliving something he had tried to bury.

Chapter Two

"Get up, Caleb! Don't make me come up there!"

The angry voice thundered through the bedroom door, but Caleb didn't move. He lay flat on his back, staring at the ceiling fan as its blades circled endlessly. He didn't want to get up. Partly because he was tired, but mostly because he hated his foster home.

He closed his eyes and wished things could go back to the way they were. When it was just him and Grandpa. His parents had died in a plane crash when he was an infant. He had no memory of them, only faint impressions pulled from the rare times Grandpa spoke of them.

Everything else, every memory that mattered, was tied to the old man. Life with Grandpa had been simple, even when money was tight. Black Mountain had always been home, and Grandpa made sure it felt that way. With his contagious laugh, quiet acts of generosity, and the kind of presence that made people feel seen, he was known and respected all over town, and no one loved him more than Caleb.

But six months ago, everything had changed. Grandpa's health had crumbled, and with it, their life together. One day, Caleb was at home; the next, he was standing in a sterile nursing home, watching the strongest man he knew fade away. And when Grandpa couldn't care for him anymore, there was nowhere else to go.

That was how he ended up here. The Williams household.

"Caleb Wilder!" the man barked again.

Caleb groaned, dragging himself upright. His long legs dangled over the edge of the bed, his toes nudging piles of dirty laundry. He snatched a wrinkled T-shirt from the floor and yanked it over his head, then shoved his legs into sweatpants he didn't bother to adjust. His fingers combed through his bedhead, trying and failing to tame it as he entered the hall.

Family portraits lined the wall, glossy smiles staring back at him. A perfect family in perfect poses, frozen in frames. The twins' hair was curled, their dresses spotless, and Richard's arm was clamped tight around Samantha's shoulders.

He almost laughed. The Williamses fooled the world with their picture-perfect lives, but Caleb knew better.

The rich smell of coffee followed him down the stairs and into the kitchen, where sunlight spilled across the polished countertops and spotless sink. Everything was neatly placed, nothing out of line. Yellow curtains framed the window, bright and welcoming as if the house itself were happy, but the family at the table drained the warmth from the room.

"Glad you could make it." Richard glanced up from his newspaper, his words sharp with sarcasm.

Caleb ignored the remark and slid into the only open seat, where an empty bowl and spoon waited for him. He kept his eyes low, avoiding the twins' glares aimed at him from across the table.

He poured himself a decent helping of cereal, topped it with milk, and tried to eat quietly.

The twins had other plans. They looked like little princesses in their matching pink outfits and white bows, but they ate like wild animals. One slurped the last drops from her bowl while the other banged her spoon as if she were in a marching band.

Caleb clenched his own spoon, his knuckles whitening as heat crawled up his neck. He focused on chewing, swallowing, breathing...anything to keep from snapping.

Because if he did, it'd only make things worse.

"Daddy, Caleb keeps kicking me!"

The newspaper hit the table with a loud slam. Caleb flinched before he could stop himself. Richard's bloodshot eyes locked onto him. "Keep your feet to yourself."

"I didn't kick her," Caleb said, his stomach twisting.

"He's lying, Daddy!"

Richard jabbed a thick finger in Caleb's direction. "I suggest you keep your mouth shut and eat your breakfast."

Caleb dropped his eyes instantly, his throat tightening as he stared at the soggy cereal. His hand shook against the spoon, but he forced it still, gripping harder until the metal dug into his palm.

Across the table, one of the twins smirked, satisfied with the chaos she'd stirred up.

Samantha sat silent at the end of the table, her mug trembling in her hands as she kept her gaze fixed on the steam rising from it. She drank slowly, pretending she hadn't seen anything, as if staying invisible might spare her from Richard's temper.

Ring! Ring!

Samantha jolted to her feet, moving toward the phone like it might bite her if she got too close.

"Who's calling this early?" Richard demanded.

"I don't recognize the number," she whispered, her hand shaking as she picked it up.

"Answer it."

"Hello?" Samantha answered. "Yes, this is his foster mother. Oh dear, we'll head that way now. Thank you." She ended the call and turned to Caleb, her expression clouded. "It's your grandfather. We need to go to the nursing home right away."

Fear slammed into Caleb. He launched out of his chair and bolted from the kitchen. Richard's voice rose at Samantha, but Caleb barely heard it. He knew only one thing: he had to get to Grandpa.

Upstairs, he grabbed a hoodie from a pile of clothes and shoved it over his head, then jammed his feet into his sneakers. He nearly tripped over himself as he tore back into the hall, praying Samantha was ready. He wasn't old enough to drive, and Richard controlled everything. Samantha was his only hope of seeing Grandpa.

When he hit the bottom of the stairs, Richard was still raging, but Samantha stood at the front door, keys in hand. She didn't look at her husband or answer him. She just opened the door and stepped into the cold.

Caleb pushed past Richard, his stomach churning, and followed her outside. The icy air burned his lungs, but Richard's glare was worse, stabbing into his back. He didn't know why Richard was so furious. Nothing ever made sense with him. But Caleb knew one thing: there'd be punishment later.

For now, he didn't care. He was going to see Grandpa.

Chapter Three

The chilly air cut through Caleb's clothes as he bolted toward the brand-new minivan parked in the driveway. He reached it first, yanking at the passenger door. It was locked.

Beep. Beep.

The lights flashed twice, and the lock clicked open.

The handle felt like ice as Caleb pulled the door open and jumped inside. The cold leather seat seeped through his sweatpants, making him shiver as he fumbled with the seatbelt. Winter had barely begun, but he was already freezing.

Samantha climbed into the driver's seat, her small frame swallowed by a heavy winter coat. Her light brown hair was down and neatly smoothed into place, but worry still tugged at her tired features. She wasn't cruel like Richard, just scared and trying to hold things together.

The van crawled through the waking neighborhood. Frost sparkled across lawns and rooftops, and cars rumbled in driveways, their exhausts curling like smoke signals. Christmas decorations still clung to porches, their colors dulled in the frost. Strings of lights drooped across roofs, half of them dark, leftover from a holiday that had already passed.

Caleb barely noticed. All he could think about was Grandpa.

Who called Samantha? he wondered. *What did they say?*

He told himself everything would be okay, but deep down he knew better. A knot of dread sat heavy in his stomach, whispering that he was about to lose the one person who truly loved him.

As his chilled body thawed in the van, tears stung his eyes and blurred the houses rolling past. He swiped them away with his sleeve, angry at himself for letting them surface. Fear pressed against his chest until he could hardly breathe. He wanted to scream, to sob, to demand that the van go faster. But instead, he sat rigid with his fists clenched, forcing himself to stay calm.

The nursing home was only ten minutes away, but the ride stretched on like hours. When the brick building finally appeared, Caleb stiffened, his shoulders locking as they turned into the semi-empty parking lot.

Unbuckling his seatbelt with trembling fingers, Caleb shoved the door open and leaped from the van before it stopped. He sprinted toward the nursing home entrance, not sparing Samantha a glance.

All that mattered was getting inside.

"Caleb, wait!" Samantha shouted as the brakes screeched.

Caleb didn't look back as he charged through the automatic doors, warmth rushing over him. Christmas was over, but everything was still decorated as if it had just begun. Paper snowflakes dangled from the ceiling, and a glowing tree stood tall in the corner with fake presents stacked beneath it.

He flew past the front desk and down the hall to his right, his lungs burning as he reached room 110.

Breathing hard, Caleb slowed as he nudged the half-open door and stepped inside. Light spilled through the window, filling a room that looked more like a hospital than the bedroom Grandpa had called home for months.

Tears welled in his eyes as he took in the frail figure propped up in bed, surrounded by wires and monitors, their steady beeping demanding attention. Caleb hardly recognized his grandfather. It had only been a couple of weeks since their last visit, yet Grandpa looked twenty pounds lighter, his shrunken frame swallowed by the sheet.

"Grandpa?" Caleb whispered, inching closer.

"Is that you, Little Wilder?" Grandpa cracked open his weary eyes, turning his head toward him.

"Yes." Caleb choked back tears. "I'm here."

"It's so great to see you." Grandpa's thin fingers closed gently around Caleb's hand before his eyes drifted shut again.

"Please don't leave me," Caleb begged, hot tears sliding down his cheeks. "You're all I have left."

"There's no escaping the inevitable," Grandpa murmured. "My time here is ending."

"No, Grandpa."

"Son, I need you to do something for me." A faint smile curved his wrinkled lips. "When I'm gone, go into my old bedroom. Under the bed, you'll find a floorboard that sits just a little higher than the rest. Pry it open and look inside. The box, and everything in it, belongs to you."

"You can't die, Grandpa." Caleb gripped his hand tighter, a sob climbing his throat. "I won't survive without you."

"Caleb, you're stronger than you know," he said, his voice fading. "Find the box, and don't be afraid. Everything you need is inside it."

Beep!

The monitors screamed a flat line, and Caleb's chest shattered. Nurses rushed in, pushing him back as they swarmed the bed.

He couldn't breathe. He only watched, wide-eyed, as they worked frantically over his grandfather. Someone started chest compressions, and the room dissolved into chaos filled with shouted commands.

After a few desperate minutes, the fight drained from their faces. A nurse met his eyes and shook her head. "I'm sorry."

"No!" Caleb screamed.

He lunged toward the bed, but another nurse caught his arm in a vicelike grip, dragging him back. His legs buckled, and he collapsed onto the cold tile, a wail ripping from his chest. He pounded the floor until his knuckles stung, screaming as if his desperation could bring his grandfather back. But the room stayed still, the monitors silent.

Grandpa was gone, and he wasn't coming back.

Chapter Four

Snow flurries pattered against the windshield of the minivan as it hurried down the icy road. Caleb sat in the passenger seat, numb, watching the endless trees rush by.

The past week had been a blur. Attending Grandpa's funeral the day before only confirmed what he feared most: he was all alone.

Beside him, Samantha drove in silence while Caleb replayed his grandfather's last words. A flicker of curiosity stirred about the mysterious box Grandpa had mentioned, but nothing inside it could ease the hopelessness strangling his soul.

The van wound its way down Pivotal Point Road, the smooth pavement giving way to gravel as it reached the driveway at the very end. The tires bounced across the uneven rocks, each bump stirring another memory in Caleb as they neared Grandpa's home.

Now that his grandfather had passed, Caleb was there to gather what he could before the house went on the market. Anything left behind would be donated.

Caleb wished he could keep everything, but he had nowhere to store it all, especially the antique furniture. He couldn't hold on to the old house and its belongings, but the five acres of land gated off behind it were now his.

He often wondered why the plot of land was so important. It had been handed down through his family since the early 1800s. Though curiosity pulled at him for years about what lay beyond the chain-link fence, he never broke his grandfather's strict rule: never enter those woods.

As the minivan slowed to a stop, Caleb's chest tightened. Icicles dangled from the roof, and for a fleeting moment he imagined Grandpa standing in the doorway, waiting for him. But the house was empty now, its peeling paint and crooked shutters a silent reminder of everything he had lost. Caleb swallowed hard, forcing back tears as he looked at the only place that had ever felt like home.

Most of his best memories were in that house, all thanks to the remarkable grandfather who was no longer there.

Samantha gave him a weak smile. "I'll wait in the car for you."

Caleb glanced her way and wondered if she had once been pretty. Wrinkles lined her face too deeply for her age, and dark circles dragged down her eyes. Living with Richard had done that. Caleb hadn't known Richard long, but it hadn't taken much time to learn what he was capable of. He wouldn't be surprised if Samantha hid the same bruises he did.

Feeling as though he was pushing through a thick haze, Caleb forced himself out of the van. The winter breeze hit him like a knife, and he shivered and hugged himself as he cautiously climbed the wobbly, ice-coated steps. On the porch, he dug under the mat for the spare key, unlocked the door, and rushed inside.

Caleb dragged his sleeve across his nose and shut the door against the icy wind. The living room was just as cold, the stale air wrapping around the worn furniture. Stepping inside felt like stepping into the past. The old kitchen table, the worn leather couch, the fireplace dark with soot. Nothing had moved.

Tears streaked down his face as he walked down the narrow hallway toward Grandpa's old bedroom. Every step felt weighted, like his shoes were made of lead. He hated what his life had become. How would he survive without Grandpa?

Why did you leave me?

Gray winter light streamed through the blinds as Caleb entered the master bedroom. Dust coated the room, untouched since Grandpa's last days. Tears burned his cheeks as he glanced at the mismatched, timeworn furniture, just as he remembered it.

The floorboards groaned as he approached the old bed, Grandpa's last words echoing in his mind. If there was a secret waiting for him, he would find it.

Dropping to his knees, he peered under the frame. All he saw was dust, but he refused to leave empty-handed.

He slid under the bedframe and swept his hands across the gritty floor, his fingers sifting through layers of filth.

Right when he was about to give up, his fingertips brushed against a board jutting half an inch higher than the rest. His pulse quickened as he traced the edges. He tugged, straining with all his strength, but the wood refused to budge. After several failed attempts, it was clear he needed something to pry it open.

Shimmying out from under the bed, Caleb rushed into the outdated kitchen and yanked a butter knife from the silverware drawer. Adrenaline surged through him as he hurried back to Grandpa's room and dove beneath the bed.

It took only seconds to find the raised board again. He jammed the knife into the crack and wiggled it until it caught. With a twist, the floorboard popped up.

His heart hammered against the floor as he tossed the knife aside and slid the wooden plank out of the way. Reaching into the dark hole, his fingers brushed something cold. A surge of excitement coursed through him as he pulled out a small metal tin and crawled out from under the bed. Without standing, he blew a layer of dust from the box and placed it in front of him.

His hands trembled as he lifted the lid and peeked inside. Resting on top was a small ring box. He plucked it out and flicked it open, his breath catching at the sight of the simple diamond ring.

He recognized it instantly. It was the same one he'd seen in old photographs of his grandmother. He'd never met her. Cancer had stolen her life before he was born, but the stories he'd grown up hearing made him feel as though he had.

Setting the ring box aside, Caleb reached into the tin again. Emotion stirred in his chest when his fingers closed around Grandpa's old golden pocket watch. He never went anywhere without it.

It was cold in his palm as he turned the watch over, the ancient device still ticking steadily. A few scratches marred the surface, but it was otherwise in good condition. Flipping it open, he studied the face before snapping the case shut again. A faint smile broke through when he saw the cursive *W* engraved on the back.

The watch had been in the Wilder family for decades, and now it was his.

Wiping away a single tear, Caleb set the pocket watch beside the ring box. He reached back into the box and pulled out a tiny key. His brows furrowed as he turned it over in his hand. He'd never seen it before and had no idea why Grandpa would leave it to him.

Caleb placed the key next to the watch before lifting out the final item: a folded note. *Little Wilder* was written across the top in black ink. It was the nickname only his grandfather had used.

Sniffling, Caleb unfolded the letter, his grief stirring at the sight of Grandpa's handwriting.

My dearest Caleb,

I want to thank you for bringing me so much joy. The years we shared together were more precious than I can ever express. After your grandmother passed, I lost all hope that things would ever get better. But oh, was I wrong. You were exactly what I needed, and I am forever grateful to you.

Although I am gone from this world, I don't want your thoughts to be consumed by my absence. You have a long life ahead of you, and I want you to enjoy it.

There is something that I have desired to share with you for quite some time, but oddly enough, I somehow knew it was not the right time. Now that I have passed, it's time to let you in on the life-changing secret that has been passed down in our family line for generations.

The forest behind our home, the one that now belongs to you, is no ordinary place. My father introduced me to it many years ago, not long before he passed away. You were only a baby then, but the forest changed my life forever. It is unlike our world and beyond anything you could possibly imagine.

The key I've left for you will unlock the gate to that enchanted place. There you will discover what your heart most desires and so much more.

Be brave, Little Wilder, and know that you are never alone, although it may feel that way at times. You are stronger than you realize, and you can overcome anything that stands in your way.

All my love,

Grandpa

Caleb read the note again and again until his tears streaked the ink into black smudges.

What was Grandpa talking about? The words felt too heavy, too strange, as if they couldn't have belonged to the man he knew. Maybe it was just the sickness talking in his last days.

Caleb folded the note with slow, careful hands and slid it into his pocket with the ring, watch, and key. Standing, he went to the window that faced the backyard.

Frost clung to the trees beyond the chain-link fence lined with "no trespassing" signs. It was the same forest Grandpa had forbidden him from entering his entire life. He hadn't been strict about much, but that one rule had been set in stone.

So why now, after all these years, would Grandpa change his mind?

The icy branches scraped against the rusted fence, swaying as if they were daring Caleb to come inside. For years, he'd wondered what lay beyond the barrier, but the thought of entering the forest made his chest constrict. The longer he stared into the snowy woods, the more he realized he wasn't brave enough to go in alone.

"Sorry, Grandpa," Caleb whispered. "I can't."

He wandered through the rooms of his childhood home, his steps growing heavier with each room. It felt like the last time he'd ever be there. Most of his things were already gone, packed up when he moved in with the Williamses. Now, all he chose to take was a single framed photo of him and Grandpa, which he carried back to the living room.

The cold air nipped at Caleb as he stepped outside, sliding the spare key back beneath the doormat. Clutching the picture frame to his chest, he braced against the wind and carefully made his way down the icy steps toward the waiting minivan.

Snow was falling harder when he climbed into the passenger seat. Heat poured from the vents, wrapping around him, but he still shivered as he shut the door and set the frame on his lap.

"Is that all you're taking?" Samantha asked, shifting the car into reverse.

"Yeah," Caleb lied. He wasn't about to tell her about the hidden box he'd found.

As the van backed out of the snowy driveway, Caleb kept his eyes fixed on the house until the trees swallowed it from sight. He wasn't sure he'd ever see it again, even though it wasn't far from where he lived now.

When they pulled into the Williamses' pristine driveway, the blast of the heater had finally started to thaw him. The place looked like something from a magazine, with fresh paint, tall windows, and perfectly trimmed hedges dusted with snow. It was beautiful, but it would never feel like home. Grandpa's house had carried more warmth than this one ever could.

Samantha hadn't said a word the entire ride, and Caleb was fine with that. He rarely spoke to her anyway and wasn't about to start now. He had too much on his mind.

They hurried from the van to the front door, the cold cutting sharper with each second.

Samantha jammed the key into the lock. "Dinner will be ready in an hour."

"I'm not hungry," Caleb muttered as he stepped inside.

A warm cinnamon-apple scent drifted through the foyer, wafting from a fresh plug-in.

Hugging the picture frame, Caleb kicked off his sneakers. The house was too calm, too quiet. The twins weren't home. They were probably at ballet. And Richard was out of town, one of the rare times the house felt bearable.

But the silence didn't bring him any peace. It only made the emptiness louder, pressing in until it felt like the walls themselves were closing around him. Hopelessness clung to him like a storm cloud as he dragged himself up the staircase. He entered his bedroom, locking the door behind him.

Pressing his back against the door, Caleb scanned the light-blue room with its high-dollar furniture and tasteful decorations. Everything was flawless, staged. Nothing like the home he'd been raised in. Nothing like Grandpa.

He set the picture frame on the nightstand, his thumb brushing over Grandpa's smiling face. The ache in his chest deepened as he collapsed onto the bed. It didn't take him long to fall asleep.

Chapter Five

"Grandpa!" Caleb shouted. "Wait!"

Caleb sprinted after his grandfather, who was trudging toward a snowy forest. No matter how loudly Caleb called, Grandpa didn't turn. He just kept moving steadily toward the thick tree line.

Panting for air, Caleb pushed harder, but he wasn't getting any closer. He looked down and panic struck.

His legs were buried in quicksand.

"Help me, Grandpa!"

The sand sucked at his feet, dragging him deeper with every frantic movement.

"Grandpa!" Caleb cried, the word tearing from his throat. "Don't leave me!"

Grandpa halted at the trees and slowly turned. A light breeze tousled his white hair as he gave Caleb a calm, almost knowing smile. "Come find me, Little Wilder," he said, his voice carrying on the wind. "You know where to look."

And then he was gone, fading into the woods as Caleb thrashed against the quicksand.

"No!"

***

Caleb shot upright, gasping for air. Sweat clung to his skin as he dragged a trembling hand across his damp forehead.

It was only a dream, he told himself.

He sank back onto the drenched pillow, his chest still rising and falling. He dreamed often, but none of them had ever felt so vivid or so real.

Closing his eyes, he tried to sleep again, but the dream replayed in an endless loop. Over and over, he saw Grandpa vanish into the forest while he stood helpless.

Finally, he'd had enough. He flicked on the lamp, dug into the pocket of his sweatpants, and emptied everything onto the nightstand. He snatched up his grandfather's note and read it repeatedly, as if the words might hold the answer he was looking for.

Grandpa clearly wanted him to go into the forest behind their old home. But why? All his life, he'd been told never to set foot in those woods. A place Grandpa had insisted was nothing but trees.

The thought of it only deepened his unease. He could get lost...and there was no telling what might lurk inside.

Caleb read the note again one last time before folding it into a tiny square. He picked up his grandfather's watch, flipped it open, and tucked the note inside. With a soft click, the lid closed.

Switching off the lamp, Caleb lay back down, wide awake, and stared at the dark ceiling above.

The idea of exploring the forest made his insides twist. He didn't want to go in there, but he'd never be able to shake what his grandfather had said unless he did.

Although he doubted there was anything special about the forest, he decided to push past his fear and check it out in the morning. Luckily, it was the weekend, so he didn't have school. Also, Richard was on a business trip and wouldn't be home for a couple of days, which worked in Caleb's favor.

Caleb squeezed his eyes shut, but his mind wouldn't turn off. It warned him to stay away from the forest. Images of everything that could go wrong flooded in: getting lost, getting attacked by an animal, or worse. Still, he had to face it.

After a long battle with his thoughts, sleep finally overtook him.

***

Caleb woke with a burst of energy. He threw off the covers as streams of early morning light filtered into his room. There was only one thing on his mind: the forest. His stomach churned, but he refused to let it stop him. He would go there today, no matter how he felt.

Wearing the same clothes from the day before, he didn't bother changing. He grabbed the pocket watch and key from his nightstand and tucked them into his pocket.

Caleb slipped out of his room and tiptoed down the hallway and stairs. At the bottom, he crossed the small foyer and opened the coat closet. He was already wearing a hoodie, but it wouldn't be enough. He grabbed his winter jacket, the one with gloves jammed in the pockets, and shoved his arms into the warm sleeves.

Samantha came out of the kitchen, a cup of coffee in hand. She was already dressed for the day, her light brown hair perfectly in place. She was clearly enjoying the rare peace and quiet while Richard was gone and the twins were still asleep.

"Where are you going?" she whispered, glancing up at the staircase.

"I'm going to ride my bike around the neighborhood," he said, slipping his feet into his sneakers.

Samantha nodded and turned back toward the kitchen. "Don't go too far."

"I won't," he said, unlocking the front door and stepping outside.

Slowly closing the door behind him, Caleb inhaled the crisp air that seemed to wake his entire body. The sky was a dull gray, heavy with the promise of snow. It wasn't falling yet, but it could start any second, so he quickened his pace.

Caleb's breath created a trail of smoke as he shoved his hands into his thick gloves and headed toward his old bicycle leaning against the garage door. He had always loved riding his bike; it was a temporary escape, a way to forget how cruel life had been to him.

Grabbing the handlebars, he steered the bike down the driveway and hopped on. It wasn't snowing, but patches of snow and thin ice still covered the ground. He swerved once but quickly steadied himself and kept going.

The cold air stung his face and made his eyes water as he pedaled down the long, empty street. His grandfather's pocket watch thumped against his thigh as he rode past rows of tidy homes and out of the neighborhood.

He looked both ways before darting across the main road and turning onto a back street. His calves burned as he reached Pivotal Point Road and sped down the paved road that led to his old home. His tires slipped on the ice a few times, but he managed to keep his balance and press onward.

Snow-covered trees zipped by as he passed the gated driveway belonging to the McThorn family. They were the wealthiest people in town, but they rarely stayed at their cabin since they owned multiple homes. He'd only seen them on that road a handful of times in all the years he'd lived there.

Caleb was freezing when he reached the end of the pavement and hit the short gravel road that led straight to his childhood home. His body rattled with every bump as he pedaled over the rocks. Finally, he slammed on the brakes, sending pebbles scattering through the air. His throat tightened as he stared up at the house he used to call home.

I can do this.

Climbing off his bike, he kicked down the stand and parked it beside the old house. He hurried around the back, stepping into the small yard coated in ice. The space was surrounded by towering trees dusted with snow as a low fog drifted through the forest beyond.

Chills slid down Caleb's spine as he forced himself toward the old gate. It looked as if it hadn't been opened in years. The fence was in terrible shape. It was rusted and falling apart in several places. Tree branches poked through the gaps, as if trying to break free from the barrier built around them.

His hands trembled as he unlocked the rusted padlock and yanked the chains from around the gate. Leaving the key in the lock, he reached into his pocket and pulled out his grandfather's watch. He needed to keep track of time and make sure he wasn't gone for too long.

It was only 7:15. He planned to be back at his foster home by 8:15 so Samantha wouldn't get suspicious.

Still shivering, Caleb tucked the pocket watch away and scanned the forest ahead. The trees stood dark and motionless beneath the gloomy sky.

Anxiety churned inside him, and for a split second, he was tempted to turn back and forget about the strange note Grandpa had left him. Every part of him wanted to run, but his dream resurfaced. He had to know what lay beyond the trees he'd grown up seeing every day. Even if it only proved that his grandfather had been delusional when he wrote the letter.

"Here goes nothing."

Shoving his hands into the pockets of his winter jacket, Caleb took his first step into the unknown.

Chapter Six

The fog clung to the trees as Caleb cautiously went deeper into the forest, following a well-worn path. A strange stillness hung in the air. It was colder than before, much colder, and the snow had vanished from the branches. Only a thin layer of frost glittered on the ground and trees. The forest looked different now that he was inside it.

Caleb slowed, scanning the trees. *Where did all the snow go?*

He could've sworn it had blanketed the branches before he entered.

Zipping his jacket to his chin, Caleb shivered as he crept down the path, his sneakers crunching over the icy earth. The trail eventually split into three narrow passageways, each lined with bare trees.

Worry spread through him as he studied each one. They all looked the same.

After a moment's hesitation, he chose the path on the right.

The path twisted between the trees, each branch glazed in frost that shimmered like glass. It was beautiful, but not enough to erase his fear. The woods were quiet. His eyes darted from tree to tree, waiting for movement that never came.

What was Grandpa talking about? He stepped over a fallen log. *There's nothing special about this place.*

The temperature continued to drop, and the fog refused to lift as he trekked deeper into the woods. His breath curled in front of him as he climbed over a slick rock, careful not to fall.

On and on he walked, but the forest only seemed to grow.

He should have reached the back fence by now. Five acres wasn't far.

But it wasn't in sight. All he saw were trees.

He let out a slow breath and turned around. He'd seen enough.

As Caleb made his way back, he kept his eyes on the worn trail. His heartbeat slowed as he strolled past the trees that were resting for the winter. He brushed his gloved hand against the rough bark of a tall oak and couldn't help but feel a flicker of disappointment. He wasn't sure what he'd expected to find, but it was more than an empty, silent forest.

A dark figure darted across the path and vanished into the fog.

Caleb's heart jolted. He spun, searching the haze, but it revealed nothing. *What was that?*

He stepped back, the crunch of ice beneath his shoes painfully loud in the silence.

Then, from the mist, a shape began to form.

Caleb froze as a coyote emerged from the fog, close enough that he could see the frost clinging to its fur. It didn't growl. It didn't move. It just stared.

He took a slow step back and lifted a shaky hand. "Stay back."

The coyote tilted its head slightly, studying him with amber eyes.

Then its expression shifted. A deep, throaty growl rumbled from the coyote as it stalked forward, its teeth now exposed.

Panic flooded Caleb as he backed away. He stumbled over an icy root, catching himself against a tree. His eyes darted to the ground, desperate for something—anything—to defend himself. A fallen branch stuck out from the frost. He grabbed it and gripped it like a bat.

"Go away!" he shouted, his breath coming fast and shallow.

The coyote's growl deepened as it crept closer.

Caleb swung the stick, but only hit air. The animal flinched, then lunged, clamping onto the branch and snapping it in half with a loud crack.

Caleb stumbled again, his heart hammering. The broken piece slipped from his shaking hands.

The coyote's breath fogged the air as it inched forward, its fangs bared.

Then the ground shook.

A low rumble rolled through the forest, followed by the heavy rhythm of hooves pounding the frozen earth. The coyote paused, its ears flicking toward the sound.

Out of the fog came a massive shape. At first it was a shadow, then a horse. It burst through the mist, its coat black as coal with dark blue streaked through its mane and tail. Steam rose from its nostrils with every snort.

Atop the horse sat a young man dressed in jeans and a tan jacket. He looked to be in his early twenties, with long chestnut hair and a thick beard. A sword hung at his side, swaying lightly as the horse came to a halt.

Caleb's breath hitched. A person was the last thing he expected to see on his land.

The stranger swung down, his boots striking the ground with a dull thud.

The coyote turned around, its focus shifting from Caleb to the newcomer. It lowered itself, its lips peeling back in a silent snarl.

The man stepped forward and drew his sword. The hiss of metal cut through the fog. Caleb flinched at the sound, the hairs on his neck rising.

A sword? Why does he have a sword?

People carried handguns nowadays, not medieval weapons.

The stranger pointed the sharp blade at the coyote.

The animal's eyes flicked from the sword to the man's face. Its growl faltered. For a heartbeat, the forest held its breath. Then it showed its teeth once more before darting into the mist, vanishing as quickly as it had appeared.

The young man sheathed his weapon and turned to Caleb.

Caleb stood rigid, his breath coming in short bursts. He was tall for fifteen, nearly six feet, but the man was taller. And stronger. Caleb's lanky build couldn't compare to the man's lean, powerful frame.

The stranger approached slowly, the fog parting around him. He extended a hand, a faint, reassuring smile crossing his face. "My name's Jesse."

"Caleb." He shook Jesse's calloused hand awkwardly.

"Nice to meet you, Caleb," Jesse said, his smile brightening.

Caleb managed a small nod, though confusion tugged at him. What was Jesse doing on his land? No one had access to the property—or at least, he didn't think so. Maybe Grandpa had given him permission before he passed.

Caleb finally looked up. Jesse's face was ordinary enough, but his eyes were captivating. The astonishing shade of green caught him off guard. They gleamed like polished emeralds and carried a kindness Caleb rarely saw.

The ground vibrated as the massive horse stomped up to them. He stood like a wall, towering over Caleb, his muscles rippling beneath a coat as black as night. Streaks of deep blue shimmered faintly through his mane, catching what little light the forest offered.

Blue? In its mane?

It was odd, but it didn't diminish the animal's power.

Caleb swallowed hard; he'd never stood so close to something so powerful. Plus, he had no experience with horses. They'd always intimidated him. Especially this one.

"This is Regal," Jesse said, patting the horse's side. "You can pet him if you want. He won't hurt you."

Caleb backed away, shaking his head. "I'm good."

"No problem." He ran a hand through the horse's mane. "I'm headed to my cabin to warm up. Want to tag along?"

Caleb raised his brows. Grandpa had never mentioned a cabin on their land. *Is this another secret he kept from me?*

"You have a cabin here?" Caleb asked.

Jesse shook his head. "No. It's beyond the forest."

Caleb exhaled, relief washing through him, though confusion lingered. His entire property was supposed to be gated off. At least, that was what Grandpa had always told him. Maybe the back wasn't. That could explain how Jesse had wandered in. It still didn't make sense, but at least Jesse wasn't living on his land. That would have only made things more complicated.

"It's not too far from here," Jesse added.

A strange warmth pooled in Caleb's stomach. He'd always been told never to talk to strangers, never to trust them, and definitely never to follow them. But Jesse didn't feel like a stranger. Caleb couldn't explain it, but for the first time since his grandfather passed, he felt safe. Like he'd known Jesse his whole life.

"I'd better head back before my foster mom starts to worry," Caleb said.

"Okay. I'll show you the way out," Jesse said, grabbing the reins.

Regal snorted softly as Jesse led him down the path. The thick fog still clung to the trees, completely unbothered by their passing. Caleb walked beside him, his thoughts tangled somewhere between caution and curiosity. Every few steps, he risked another glance at the young man who'd come out of nowhere.

Jesse walked with an easy confidence Caleb didn't have, his long, wavy hair swaying with each stride. Even in the cold, he didn't seem to shiver. His steps were deliberate, as if he knew exactly where he was going.

"Thanks for helping me," Caleb whispered, wiping his runny nose with his gloved hand.

"You're welcome," Jesse said, glancing at him before looking back at the trail.

They didn't say much as they walked, but Caleb was fine with that. Peace settled over him as Regal's hooves thudded beside him. It was strange but relaxing, a feeling he hadn't experienced in months. He'd grown so used to the chaos that he'd almost forgotten what peace felt like.

The fog was still thick and heavy when Jesse finally stopped. Through the haze, Caleb could barely make out his old backyard beyond the gate.

He found it odd that Jesse knew exactly where he'd come from, but he didn't ask. He didn't want to know.

"Here's your stop, Caleb." Jesse tipped his bearded chin toward the fence. "If you ever want to explore, I'd love to show you around."

Show me around? Caleb frowned. The guy talked like he owned the place. Maybe he didn't realize it was private property. And Caleb wasn't about to point it out.

He stepped forward but paused at the gate, his hand resting on the chain. "If I come back, how will I find you?"

　　　　　　　　　　　

"All you have to do is look," Jesse said, a faint smile touching his lips. He turned Regal around and led him back into the forest until they both disappeared into the mist like ghosts. Caleb stood there, staring into the icy trees as Jesse's words echoed in his mind.

What is he talking about?

Now that he was alone again, the peace he'd felt began to fade. Anxiety crept in, gnawing at his chest as he pushed through the gate and stepped into his old backyard. He retrieved the key from the lock and pocketed it before wrapping the chain around the entrance and securing it tightly.

He pulled out his pocket watch to check the time. Opening the golden case, he brushed aside the small, folded note inside. Confusion flared when the clock face still read 7:15.

He frowned and gave it a shake. It was still ticking, but the hands hadn't moved.

It must need new batteries.

Moments like this made him wish he still had his cellphone. Richard had taken it the day he moved in, and he hadn't seen it since. Hopefully, he'd get it back soon.

With a quiet huff, he closed the golden case and returned it to his pocket. Then he jogged through the frost-covered grass toward the front of the house, his breath clouding in the cold air.

His thoughts swirled as he grabbed his bike by the handlebars and guided it down the bumpy gravel driveway until he reached the pavement.

Hopping on, he pedaled down the slick road as fast as he could without wrecking. He had no idea how long he'd been gone, only that he needed to hurry. The cold wind slapped against his face as he rode. He desperately hoped Samantha hadn't noticed his long absence.

Within minutes, he reached the fancy neighborhood and the two-story house he was stuck in. He skidded into the driveway and leaned his bike against the garage door before sprinting up the steps.

Caleb took a slow breath, then slipped inside and shut the door behind him. The heat of the house wrapped around him, but something felt off. It was silent. He'd expected the twins to be up by now.

Kicking off his sneakers, Caleb shoved his gloves into his jacket pockets before hanging it in the closet. He walked down the hallway into the kitchen that smelled like coffee and toasted bread.

Samantha sat alone at the table, sipping her morning brew. She looked up as he entered. "You're back already?"

"Yeah." Caleb grabbed a water bottle from the fridge and took a quick sip.

"That was a really short ride."

Caleb lowered the bottle slowly. "What?"

Samantha pointed to the clock on the wall. "You left at 7:10."

Caleb stared at the clock. Its hands pointed to 7:20.

Ten minutes? That can't be right.

The bottle trembled in his hand.

It only took about five minutes to ride his bike to his childhood home. So what happened to the rest of the time? He hadn't been in the woods long. Maybe twenty minutes. Maybe more. It was as if time itself had stopped while he was there.

That's impossible.

Samantha stood from the table and set her empty mug in the sink. "Don't forget to do your chores," she said as she left the kitchen.

Caleb couldn't tear his eyes from the ticking clock. *Did time really stand still?*

He pinched the bridge of his nose, his thoughts spinning faster than he could keep up with. It had been a strange morning, one he'd never forget. Questions churned in his mind, but only one person could answer them: Jesse.

But how was Caleb supposed to find him?

Just thinking about returning to the woods made his gut clench. What if he ran into the coyote again? Or something worse?

Caleb wrestled with the rising fear before pushing it aside. He would go back into that forest, whether he liked it or not.

Chapter Seven

A few hours later, after finishing his chores and eating lunch, Caleb found himself once again standing before the fenced-off tree line. Now that the fog had lifted and the sun was breaking weakly through the clouds, the woods didn't seem quite as spooky.

Let's get this over with.

Caleb tightened his grip on the machete in his hand as he stepped through the gate and into the forest until he was surrounded by nothing but ice and stillness. He had no idea how to actually use the machete, but it was the only thing he'd found in the garage besides a hammer. It looked more intimidating. He figured, if nothing else, it might be enough to scare off the coyote if it decided to show up again.

The cold was just as brutal as before as Caleb followed the same path. With the fog gone, he could finally see just how vast the forest was. The trees stretched endlessly before him, a sea of bare trunks fading into the distance. There didn't seem to be an end.

His sneakers crunched over the frozen ground, the sound echoing through the empty woods while his eyes searched for any sign of Jesse.

Jesse had said he'd find him...but how?

Caleb hadn't been walking long when he heard something. He stilled, his ears straining toward a faint whistle drifting on the wind. The tune rose and fell as if beckoning him to follow. His heart thumped as he moved toward the sound, hoping it would lead him to Jesse.

The whistling grew louder as Caleb stepped off the path, following the sound through the trees. The wind stirred the branches, carrying the tune as he kept moving. He pushed past a thick evergreen and stopped cold. It wasn't Jesse. It was...an old man.

Caleb tilted his head. Another person? First Jesse, and now this guy. His property clearly wasn't as gated off as Grandpa had claimed. Or there was another way in that he wasn't aware of.

The stranger appeared to be in his seventies, his white hair shining beneath a newsboy cap. Dressed in a tweed jacket and black slacks, he looked as if he'd stepped straight out of the 1930s. He was completely out of place in the middle of the forest.

Caleb stayed hidden behind a tangle of overgrown branches that jabbed at his jacket. The old man crouched near the edge of a path, sifting through fallen twigs as he whistled softly to himself.

What is he doing?

After watching for a few minutes, Caleb crept closer while holding his breath. A dry stick beneath his shoe snapped, loud as a gunshot in the still woods.

The elderly man straightened, brushing his hands on his slacks before turning toward Caleb.

"Well, hello there," he said, his accent light and welcoming as he gave a friendly wave.

Caleb faltered for a second, embarrassed that he'd been caught spying. With no choice but to reveal himself, he stepped out from his hiding place and gave a nervous wave. "Hi."

The gentleman removed his newsboy cap and brushed a hand through his pearly-white hair as he approached. Though he was shorter than Caleb, he carried himself like a man twice his size. Fine lines creased around his honey-colored eyes, and a soft smile touched his lined face as he extended a wrinkled hand. "My name is Henry Snow."

Caleb blinked. *Snow?* He didn't know anyone by that name, and certainly no one who dressed like that. Where had he come from? And why was he on Caleb's land?

"I'm Caleb." He shifted the machete to his other hand before shaking Henry's small, weathered hand.

"Wonderful to meet you, Caleb," Henry said, nodding toward the machete. "That is quite the weapon you've got there."

Caleb glanced down awkwardly. "I was...uh...using it for protection."

"A wise decision, young lad." Henry chuckled warmly. "You never know what you might run into in these woods."

His white mustache twitched with amusement before he bent down again, picking through the sticks and twigs as though he were searching for something he'd lost. Caleb watched closely, puzzled by how out of place he looked. And that accent...Caleb couldn't place it. He clearly wasn't from around there. Still, there was something about him that felt familiar. His easy smile and gentle manner reminded Caleb of his grandfather. He couldn't explain it, but he was glad he'd found the old man.

"What are you looking for?" Caleb asked, taking a cautious step toward him.

"I dropped one of my star pins."

"Star pins?"

Henry retrieved a handful of small silver pins from the pocket of his tweed jacket. Each one was shaped like a star and about the size of a dime, ending in a sharp point.

"What are they for?"

"A project of mine," Henry said with a grin.

Caleb's brows furrowed. What kind of project needed little silver stars? It didn't make any sense, but curiosity got the better of him. He stabbed the machete into the dirt and crouched beside Henry. "I'll help you look."

Henry's face lit up. "That would be wonderful."

Together, they searched the forest floor, moving branches and tossing aside sticks that got in their way. Caleb's gloves were filthy in no time, and after several minutes of searching, a faint glimmer caught his eye near his shoe.

He reached down and plucked the star from the dirt. Wiping it on his sweatpants, he stood and held it out to Henry. "I found it."

"Well done!" Henry plucked the star pin from Caleb's hand and moved to the closest oak tree near the path. Pressing the pin into the rough bark, he stepped back to admire his work, then glanced over his shoulder at Caleb. "What do you think?"

Caleb leaned in, squinting at the trunk. The small silver star almost disappeared against the bark. "Why'd you do that?"

"I am making a trail," he said, his voice bright with excitement. "I've been placing these stars in certain trees to mark a path."

Caleb went quiet. *A path? On my land?* Maybe the old man was lost. Or maybe he'd known Grandpa. It would explain why he seemed so comfortable out there, and why Jesse had too. Whatever the reason, Caleb was too afraid to ask.

"A path to where?" he asked instead.

"Ah, that's the fun part. You'll have to follow it to find out. Would you like to help me?"

Caleb shifted his weight. Henry's kindness felt genuine, but there was something unusual about him. Something he couldn't place. He wanted to find Jesse, but he also wanted to stay with Henry. Maybe he could continue his search afterward.

Caleb shrugged. "I guess."

"Excellent," Henry said, tipping a few pins into Caleb's hand. "This way, Caleb. We have a path to make."

Caleb pulled the machete from the earth and trailed after Henry down the narrow path. Every instinct told him it was risky to follow a stranger into the woods, but fear never came. Instead, a strange familiarity settled over him, as if Henry were an old friend.

As they walked, Henry occasionally paused beside certain trees and let Caleb press a star pin into the rough bark. It was a simple task, yet Caleb found himself enjoying it more than he expected.

"Who is this trail for?" Caleb asked, sticking another star in place.

"For anyone who loses their way."

Caleb gave Henry a puzzled look, but the old man didn't elaborate. He simply moved on to the next tree, humming softly as he went. Caleb followed, still unsure what Henry meant. He knew by now they were far past his property line. There should've been a fence or gate somewhere, but there wasn't. Only more forest. The thought unsettled him, but he ignored it and kept walking.

The longer he walked beside Henry, the more at ease he felt. At his foster home, he was always on edge, waiting for the next argument or slammed door. But here, with Henry, that weight seemed to fade. His kindness made Caleb feel something he hadn't in a long time...safe. It was the same way Jesse made him feel.

After Caleb pressed the last star into the bark of a sturdy tree, he realized the dirt path had ended. Beyond the tree line stretched an open clearing. It was lush and impossibly green. Flowerbeds spilled across the grass, their colors rich and vibrant, beneath towering trees draped in thick, full leaves.

Caleb squinted as the cold air nipped at his nose. Everything looked and smelled like spring, even though it was winter. Birds chirped from somewhere unseen as he lifted a hand to shield his eyes from the sudden sunshine.

In the center of the clearing sat a log cabin, with smoke curling from its chimney. It was only one story, yet it stood out against the beauty surrounding it.

Caleb scanned the clearing again. The scene was almost too perfect, like something from a dream.

"We are finished," Henry said, folding his hands behind his back. "Thank you for your help."

Caleb kept his eyes on the view, unable to look away. "You're welcome."

"That's my place." Henry looked toward the cabin. "Would you like to come inside and warm up?"

Caleb hesitated. He needed to find Jesse. That was the whole point of him entering the forest. But there was something about the cabin that pulled at him. It felt warm, inviting, and even mysterious. If the outside was this breathtaking, he could only imagine what waited inside.

One look wouldn't hurt. And then he could begin his search for Jesse.

"Okay," he said.

"Fantastic!" Henry stepped out of the woods. "Follow me."

Chapter Eight

Caleb stepped into the clearing beside Henry Snow, the soft grass bending beneath their shoes. Thousands of flowers painted the yard in every color imaginable, swaying gently in the wind as if alive. He passed one flowerbed after another, the sweet scent thick in the air as he breathed it in.

The closer they came to the cabin, the more unreal it all felt. The porch wrapped around the home, its rocking chairs moving lightly in the breeze as the wind chimes played a soft, pleasant tune.

Tension coiled in Caleb as he gripped the machete tighter. He followed Henry up the steps, his chest pounding as the door opened.

"Welcome to my home," Henry said, widening the door as he entered.

Caleb lingered in the doorway before following Henry in. The sweet smell of apple cider greeted him at once. A fire crackled softly in the stone fireplace, its heat brushing against his chilled cheeks. He glanced around the spacious room that was filled with warm light and cozy, well-crafted furniture.

What caught his attention most was the kitchen. It was a wide, open space with a massive island at its center.

His thoughts instantly went to Grandpa. They'd cooked together for as long as he could remember, working side by side in the kitchen. Those were some of his best memories.

The thought stung, filling him with a sudden sadness. He hadn't cooked a single thing since moving into his foster home. And he knew he never would.

"Hey there, Caleb."

Caleb nearly jumped out of his skin when he spun and saw Jesse rising from the leather couch. Jesse set his book aside and came toward him, wearing a plaid shirt and jeans.

"Hey," Caleb said, his heart still thumping.

He'd found him. Without even trying. He couldn't believe it.

"Great to see you again." Jesse gave him a friendly handshake. "Let me get your coat."

Caleb stood rooted to the floor, mind spinning. He didn't know what to say. Didn't know how to bring up the time slip.

The silence stretched. Maybe he could stay a few minutes and bring it up later.

With a plan in mind, Caleb leaned his machete against the log wall before pulling off his gloves and shoving them into his coat pocket. Then he slipped out of his jacket and handed it to Jesse, watching as he hung it on the rack by the door.

"I'm so glad you're home, Jesse." Henry gave him a light clap on the shoulder. "That fire feels wonderful."

"Nothing beats a warm fire on a cold day," Jesse said, turning toward the kitchen. "There's apple cider on the stove; I'll pour you both a cup."

"Thank you," Henry said before beaming at Caleb. "Come on. Let's relax by the fire."

The cabin was warm and welcoming, but Caleb couldn't shake his nerves. He was surrounded by strangers in a place that felt too peaceful to trust. Part of him wanted to leave, but something in him wanted to stay.

His palms were slick with sweat as he followed Henry toward the fireplace and eased onto the leather couch. He sat stiffly, his fingers fidgeting in his lap while Henry settled onto the other sofa.

"Would you like to play a game?" Henry asked.

Caleb gave Henry a surprised look. He loved games, maybe even more than football. And that said a lot coming from a quarterback.

He used to spend hours playing checkers and cards with Grandpa. Those evenings had always been special. But he couldn't remember the last time he'd played a game with anyone.

Since moving in with the Williams family, he'd lost most of his friends. Part of it was Richard never letting him go out, but part of it was him. He'd grown withdrawn, weighed down by everything he hated about his life.

The happy, outgoing Caleb felt long gone, replaced by a version of himself he barely recognized.

He'd even quit Boy Scouts, something he'd stuck with for years, because Richard made it clear that Caleb didn't belong to anything that wasn't under his control. Football was the only thing Richard hadn't taken from him, and Caleb hoped it stayed that way.

"I guess," Caleb said.

"Splendid." Henry tapped his knees before leaning over the coffee table. He tugged on a small handle, and a hidden drawer slid open. It was packed with all sorts of games. He reached for a deck of cards resting on top and set it neatly on the table.

"I love games," Jesse said, stepping in with two steaming mugs in hand.

"Did someone say games?" a cheerful voice called from the hall.

Caleb stiffened at the unexpected voice. Unease passed through him as he looked toward the hallway beside the fireplace, where heavy footfalls grew louder. He hadn't realized someone else was there.

A large man in his mid-fifties stepped into view, and Caleb's eyes widened. He was tall and heavyset with bushy red hair that nearly brushed the top of the doorway. Despite his size, his warm grin and kind eyes made him look like a redheaded Santa Claus.

"Caleb, this is my dad, Godfrey," Jesse said, his hands still full as he nodded toward his father.

"Pleasure to meet you, Caleb." Godfrey smiled, a small gap showing between his teeth as he extended his hand.

Caleb's stomach flipped as Godfrey's large hand engulfed his. The shake was firm but gentle. Fine wrinkles framed bright blue eyes so full of joy that Caleb couldn't look away.

They were so vivid, so pure, that he wondered if they were real or just colored contacts. Whatever the case, Godfrey's presence sent Caleb's heart racing, pounding so hard he thought it might burst from his chest.

"May I join you?" Godfrey asked, motioning to the spot beside Caleb.

Caleb didn't trust himself to speak. He only managed to nod, which was all the invitation Godfrey needed. The man's big belly bounced as he lowered himself into the seat. Caleb sat frozen, his insides twisting relentlessly. He couldn't make sense of what was happening to him.

"Here you go, Caleb," Jesse said, handing him a hot cup of apple cider. "I'll get you some too, Dad."

"Thank you," Godfrey replied.

Caleb cradled the mug between his palms, its warmth seeping into his skin while his heart refused to settle. He tried to ignore the strange rush of emotions as he lifted the cider to his lips.

Caleb blew lightly across the surface before taking a small sip. The rich sweetness burst across his tongue, taking him by surprise. It was so good that he took another quick sip as Jesse returned to the living room.

Jesse handed his father a steaming cup of cider before settling beside Henry, who was happily sipping his own.

"Smells amazing," Godfrey said, the steam curling around his face as he took a sip.

Caleb still couldn't believe that Godfrey and Jesse were related. They looked nothing alike—different builds, different skin tones, even their hair couldn't have been more different.

Maybe Jesse is adopted.

Caleb glanced between them again. Either way, they shared the same easygoing personality that made them easy to like.

As Caleb sipped his drink, he couldn't shake the strange pull he felt toward Godfrey. He didn't know this man, yet everything in him wanted to. The feeling only deepened the longer he sat beside him.

Caleb placed his warm mug on the end table, careful not to bump the lamp, while Jesse pulled the coffee table closer to the couches. Jesse grabbed the deck of cards resting in the center and began to shuffle.

"What should we play?" Jesse asked, the cards snapping in his hands.

"You can never go wrong with rummy or war," Henry said before taking another sip.

"Or spades," Jesse added.

Godfrey looked over at Caleb. "What would you like to play?"

Heat rushed to his cheeks as all eyes turned to him. His favorite card game was poker, but he was too nervous to admit it. Grandpa had taught him to play when he was ten, and he'd loved it ever since. They never played for money, but it was still fun.

"I don't care," Caleb said with a shrug.

"Let's play Texas Hold'em," Godfrey said, a knowing smile tugging at his lip.

Caleb's head jerked up. It was as if Godfrey had read his mind. He hadn't just picked poker; he'd named Caleb's favorite version of it.

"Great idea." Jesse split the deck and continued to shuffle.

Excitement flickered through Caleb, but it quickly died when he realized he didn't have any money. Most people only played when cash was on the line.

Fear crawled up Caleb's neck as Jesse opened the hidden drawer in the coffee table and grabbed a set of poker chips. His mind reeled, desperate for an excuse. He shifted in his seat, the weight of embarrassment pressing down on him.

Anxiety tightened his chest as Jesse dealt out stacks of poker chips, each one a different color. He wanted to say something, anything, but his throat was locked tight. When Jesse finished, Caleb finally forced the words out.

"Actually...I, uh, don't want to play that."

Godfrey tilted his head. "Why not?"

Caleb hesitated, struggling for an answer.

"Don't worry, Caleb," Godfrey said gently. "We're not playing for money. Just for fun."

Caleb narrowed his eyes. He hadn't said anything about money.

"Come now." Godfrey straightened his stack of chips. "Let's have some fun."

Caleb opened his mouth to protest, then stopped as the tension in his chest began to ease. He wasn't sure why. Maybe it was Godfrey's calm tone. Or maybe, for once, he just wanted to let his guard down and enjoy himself.

Caleb exhaled slowly and reached for a dark blue chip. He rolled it between his fingers. The smooth weight of it brought a small smile to his lips. It felt good. Familiar. For a second, he could almost see Grandpa sitting across the table from him.

Jesse shuffled the deck one last time and dealt two cards to each of them. The fire popped softly in the background as Caleb slid the blue chip back into its stack and lifted the corner of his cards.

Two kings. His pulse quickened. *So far, so good.*

Jesse turned over the first three cards in the middle of the table. Another king stared back at him. Caleb's breath caught. Three of a kind. Not perfect, but good enough to win.

They went around the table. Henry folded early, but Jesse matched Caleb's bet, and so did Godfrey.

The next card didn't help, but Godfrey's eyes lit up as he tossed in a handful of chips.

Jesse watched his dad for a few seconds, then sighed and pushed his cards away. "Fold."

Godfrey grinned at Caleb. "Your move."

Caleb studied the table, then slid more chips into the pot. "I'll raise you."

A deep laugh rolled out of Godfrey as he matched the bet. "This is turning into an exciting first round."

Jesse flipped the final card. A jolt shot through Caleb. Another king.

He tried to keep his face neutral as he tossed in a few more chips.

"Call," Godfrey said, sliding his red chips into the pile.

Caleb turned over his cards. "Four of a kind."

Godfrey revealed his own hand: a flush. Close, but not close enough.

Caleb's grin broke through before he could stop it. He reached forward, gathering the mountain of chips as laughter filled the room.

"Well played, Caleb," Godfrey said, clapping him on the back.

Caleb couldn't stop smiling. It had been a long time since he'd felt this alive. The glow of the fire, the laughter, the easy flow of the game…it almost felt like home again.

Caleb was still arranging his winnings when the next hand was dealt. He glanced at his new cards and fought to keep a straight face. It was going to be another good round.

Chapter Nine

THE SMELL OF POPCORN still hung in the air as Caleb sank deeper into the couch, watching the flames dance in the fireplace. He'd won the entire game of Texas Hold'em after hours of nonstop playing.

Since Henry had been knocked out first, he'd filled the coffee table with an assortment of snacks. Most of them were already gone.

"You are quite the poker player, young man," Godfrey said, grabbing another handful of pretzels.

"I agree," Jesse added as he tucked the poker chips and cards away.

"Thanks." A crooked grin slipped free. He hadn't had that much fun in a really long time.

Caleb looked out the window. The dreary clouds made it hard to tell how late it was. He needed to head back to his foster home before Samantha started to worry. A mix of dread and sadness washed over him. He hadn't meant to stay so long.

Then it hit him.

The time slip.

He opened his mouth, then slammed it shut. Asking it out loud suddenly felt like the dumbest thing in the world. He'd ask Jesse later. Alone. When it wouldn't sound so stupid.

"I should probably go," Caleb said.

"Nonsense." Henry waved his wrinkled hand. "You must stay for dinner."

"I can't," Caleb said, shaking his head. "My foster mom will wonder where I am."

Henry exchanged an amused glance with Godfrey before looking back at Caleb. "You don't know where you are, do you?"

"What do you mean?" Caleb asked, glancing around. "I'm at your cabin."

"That's not what I meant," he said. "Didn't you read your grandfather's letter?"

Caleb stilled, his pulse kicking hard. He'd never mentioned his grandfather...or the note he'd left him. "You...you knew my grandfather?" he asked, his voice shaky.

Henry nodded, his expression softening. "Yes. He was a dear friend of ours. We are so sorry for your loss."

Caleb's thoughts spun. They'd been friends with his grandfather. Why hadn't Grandpa told him about them? They used to tell each other everything. Or so he thought.

"He never mentioned you guys," Caleb said in a whisper.

"He mentioned you quite often," Godfrey said, folding his hands atop his round belly.

"Why didn't he tell me?"

"He didn't think you were ready."

"Ready for what?"

"This world."

Caleb frowned. "What are you talking about?"

"You're no longer in your world, Caleb," Godfrey said, mischief glinting in his gaze. "Each time you step through the gate, you cross into another realm. One that is unlike yours."

The mysterious note Grandpa had left him flashed through his mind—about the forest, the key, and a world unlike anything he could imagine. "I'm...not in Black Mountain?"

"Nope." Godfrey regarded him steadily. "You're in our realm."

Another world? Caleb raked his fingers through his dirty-blond hair as his mind swirled. *That can't be true.*

"How do I know you're telling me the truth?" Caleb asked.

Godfrey smiled softly, the firelight catching his bright blue eyes. "Didn't you find it odd that your grandfather's pocket watch didn't move while you were in here earlier?"

Caleb went still. He hadn't breathed a word about the watch. Not to any of them. "How did you know that?"

Godfrey's smile widened. "Check your watch, Caleb."

Caleb's fingers shook as he pulled it out. The hands hadn't moved. Not since he'd crossed the gate.

"Time in your world freezes the moment you enter the gated forest," Godfrey continued. "It won't start again until you return."

"That can't be true." Caleb shook his head. "I own that plot of land. It's nothing but woods."

"It's not just woods, Caleb. It's a doorway to this world," Godfrey said. "Your ancestors were the ones who found this realm and gated it off long ago."

Understanding struck Caleb all at once.

The note. The watch. The flowers blooming in winter.

Caleb stared at the unmoving hands of the pocket watch, his heart hammering against his ribs. Another world. He was in another world.

His stomach twisted. The room tilted. Nothing made sense. Time freezing? A hidden realm? His ancestors guarding a gateway? It felt impossible. It was too big, too wild, too far from anything he knew.

"How is this possible?" His voice cracked.

Godfrey patted him on the shoulder. "All things are possible here."

Caleb pressed a shaking hand to his forehead as his thoughts spiraled out of control. All these years, a secret realm had been just beyond his backyard. And Grandpa had hidden it from him. But why?

Godfrey spoke again. "Life isn't always going to be hard, Caleb."

"Easy for you to say." Caleb stared into the fire.

Godfrey studied him for a long moment. "I know more about your life than you realize."

"Like what?"

"Like Richard," Godfrey said quietly.

Caleb's head snapped toward him. There was no way Grandpa could've told him about Richard. Caleb had been placed in foster care the same day Grandpa went to the nursing home. "How do you know about him?"

A hint of mystery glimmered in Godfrey's eyes. "You'll come to find that we are not like anyone you've ever met."

Caleb swallowed hard. That much was becoming obvious. Even though he hadn't known these men long, he could tell they weren't normal. They were not only incredibly kind and joyful, but they also carried a strange peace. One that felt too good to be true.

Caleb looked at Godfrey, hoping he'd explain himself. But instead, Godfrey rose from the couch and motioned for Caleb to follow. "Come with me. I want to show you something."

Caleb froze, nerves twisting in his gut. He liked Godfrey, but trust didn't come easy. Not anymore. He prayed he wasn't making a mistake as he rose to follow.

They stepped into a wide hallway, and Godfrey turned into a doorway on the left. Caleb stopped at the threshold.

Even with the dreary weather outside, a soft glow bathed the room, revealing a charming bedroom. A plaid comforter stretched across the bed, soft and featherlike, and a plush recliner sat beside a bookshelf overflowing with books. The whole room felt cozy and inviting, like a peaceful lodge tucked deep in the mountains.

"Why did you bring me in here?" he asked, his words tight.

Godfrey gave him a small, kind smile. "I know living with the Williams family isn't easy for you. If you ever need a break or just want to get away for a while...you're always welcome to stay here."

"Here? In your cabin?" Caleb stared, certain he'd misheard him.

"Yes. We have several spare bedrooms," Godfrey said, gesturing to the room. "This one is my favorite, and it's yours anytime you want it. No strings attached."

Caleb fidgeted with the hem of his shirt, staring down at the hardwood floor. "Richard would never let me spend the night here."

"If you did spend the night, Richard would never know," Godfrey said. "Time in your world stops when you enter this realm. When you return, not a single second will have passed."

Caleb shuffled his feet, still overwhelmed by the whole thing. "Why are you being so nice to me?"

"Everyone deserves kindness," Godfrey replied. "Even you."

Emotion rushed over Caleb so fast that he nearly choked on it. He stepped into the room, brushing his fingers along the spines of the books before touching the soft comforter. It felt like a safe haven, something he hadn't had in a very long time.

He turned back to Godfrey, who greeted him with a reassuring smile.

"No one will bother you here, Caleb. You're safe with us."

Caleb sniffed and wiped his nose on his sleeve, unsure how to respond. He wasn't used to this...not since Grandpa was alive.

The sound of footsteps echoed from the hallway. Henry appeared in the doorway, wiping his hands on a dish towel. "I'm making lasagna. Would you like to help?"

A rush of excitement hit Caleb. He hadn't expected that. He really wanted to cook, more than anything, but his excitement was quickly choked by insecurity. What if he messed up? What if he embarrassed himself? It had been so long since he'd cooked anything.

Caleb lowered his head. As much as he wanted to say yes, he couldn't. "No, thanks," he mumbled.

"Come now. It will be fun." Henry's brown eyes sparkled as he stepped inside. "We both know you're a fantastic cook."

Caleb's cheeks warmed as a shy smile broke through. Grandpa must've told him. "Okay. I'll help."

"Wonderful!" Henry exclaimed as he spun around. "Come along, then—we've got dinner to make!"

Chapter Ten

Adeline sat still, her heart sinking as she stared at Caleb. He looked ahead, his gaze unfocused as if he were watching something only he could see.

"That day changed everything." He went quiet for a while, rubbing his thumb along his mug. "After that, I kept coming back. As often as I could. This cabin...it became the only place I ever felt okay."

Adeline couldn't find her voice at first. She held back tears, feeling the weight of his loneliness and pain as though it were her own. "I'm sorry about your grandfather," she whispered.

Caleb pressed his lips together as he set his coffee on the end table before leaning back into the couch. He didn't look at her, just stared ahead like he was still trapped somewhere in the past.

"How long were you in foster care?" she asked carefully.

"I guess I'm technically still in it."

"What do you mean?"

"I was living with the Williamses last time I entered this realm," he said. "I was a senior in high school and planned on moving out as soon as I graduated."

"You had to stay with Richard?"

"Yep."

A heaviness filled Adeline. She couldn't imagine living in a place like that. But then another thought struck her. Caleb had been coming here years before she'd ever stepped through the gate. And he'd been trapped in that realm for a long stretch of time, while she'd been able to come and go.

"If time stops when we're here..." She frowned. "How was I able to leave and come back...while you were stuck in the Dark Territory?"

Caleb flicked her a quick glance before looking away. "I don't know. You're the first person I've met from our world."

None of it made sense, and the longer she dwelled on it, the more confused she became. She could easily ask Godfrey or Henry through her thoughts, but she quickly dismissed it. She couldn't ask them. Not after what she had done to Jesse.

Sorrow and guilt reared their ugly heads again, but she quickly shoved the feelings down. She couldn't go there. Not now.

"What school did you go to?" she asked.

"Stone Creek," he said. "You?"

"Black Mountain High."

He huffed softly. "Rivals." His lips twitched before the faint humor faded. "Feels like a lifetime ago."

Silence settled between them again.

"I remember when your family bought my childhood home," he said.

Adeline fought back a grin as she pictured the first time she'd laid eyes on that old, shabby house. She'd hated everything about it back then, never knowing that it would lead her to her greatest blessing.

"I do too," she said. "I was not happy about it."

Caleb cracked a small smile. "It's definitely outdated, but not that bad."

"It wasn't just the house," she said. "I had to leave my home at the beach."

"Why'd you move?"

"My dad died in a car accident," she said, looking down at her lap. "My mom wanted us to be close to family."

"I'm sorry," he whispered. "That sucks."

"It's okay." She shrugged. "It led me here."

Caleb nodded, but his eyes had already drifted away. "I'll never forget when you moved in. It was around the same time I met Molly."

"Who's Molly?"

"My girlfriend."

And just like that, he was gone again.

Chapter Eleven

The bonfire roared, sparks snapping against the starry night as laughter and shouting filled the field. Caleb stood near the fire with his teammates, soaking in the heat while the rush of the win still buzzed through him.

Their football team had just won the biggest game of the season, and the coach had thrown a bonfire to celebrate. Junior year was going better than expected, especially now that he was the starting quarterback.

"Caleb!" someone called.

He turned as the cheer captain jogged over, dragging a girl along by the sleeve of her jacket. Her straight blonde hair was pulled into a neat ponytail, the cheer bow bright against the night. She was petite and pretty, small against his six-foot frame.

"This is Molly Springs; she just transferred here," the captain said. "Molly, this is our quarterback, Caleb Wilder."

Molly smiled first, quick and a little nervous. "Nice to meet you."

"Yeah...uh, you too," Caleb said, scratching the back of his neck.

The cheer captain grinned, clearly pleased with herself. "I'll let you two talk," she said before disappearing into the crowd.

Caleb cleared his throat. "So, where'd you transfer from?"

"Raleigh," Molly said. "My dad took a new job."

"That's rough."

"Yeah," she said, slipping her hands into her cheer jacket. "This place is *very* different from the city."

"I bet."

For a moment, neither of them spoke. The fire popped beside them, smoke curling upward as its warmth pushed back the October chill. Country music spilled from a nearby truck, blending with distant laughter. It was loud, but the space between them felt strangely still.

"I can show you around sometime," Caleb said, the words tumbling out before he could second-guess them. "I mean...if you want."

Molly smiled again, slower this time. "I'd like that."

Caleb looked away for a second, fighting the grin tugging at his mouth. Something unfamiliar stirred in his chest.

Football had always come first. He'd never given anything else a real chance. He'd never wanted to.

Until now.

***

The cold morning air burned Caleb's cheeks as he pedaled faster, his breath rising in quick bursts. Autumn leaves burst with color along the road as he leaned into the turn, the branches glowing in the early light. He sped up, the street sign for Pivotal Point Road flashing past as he headed toward his old property.

He had his driver's license, but no vehicle. The bike would have to do until he saved up enough for one. His phone buzzed in his pocket as he pedaled on, and the corner of his mouth lifted. He didn't need to check to know who it was.

Molly.

He'd gotten her number the night before, and they'd been texting all morning.

Nervous excitement fluttered in his stomach as he thought about their next hangout.

Then he saw the house.

Caleb slammed on the brakes, his tires skidding as the air rushed from his lungs.

There was a car in the driveway and lights on in the house.

His chest seized as he stared, rooted in place. *This can't be happening.*

The property had sat empty for years. Long enough that he'd believed that it always would be. Why would someone buy it now?

Caleb stayed frozen on his bike, his thoughts tangling. How would he enter the gate without being seen? What if he got caught? What would he say?

Anxiety crept in as he tightened his grip on the handlebars. The other realm was no longer something he could easily slip into unnoticed. Every visit would be a risk.

But walking away wasn't an option.

The friends at the cabin were his family, the only place he felt safe. It would be more complicated now, but somehow he'd make it work.

The front door burst open. A middle-aged woman with brown curls stepped outside, bundled against the cold with a purse slung over her shoulder. Panic flared. Caleb darted into the trees with his bike, pushing far enough back to stay hidden.

Two teenage girls followed her down the steps and climbed into the Bronco parked in the driveway. He was too far away to get a good look at either of them.

Caleb ducked behind a tree as the vehicle backed out and disappeared down the road.

"Now's my chance," he whispered.

Leaving his bike hidden in the woods, Caleb sprinted into the backyard, his hunting knife jarring against his hip. He unlocked the gate with shaky hands and slipped through. He pulled it shut behind him, looping the chain back into place and securing the lock.

Time had always stood still while he was there. But what if one day it didn't? He couldn't risk it, especially with the newcomers.

From now on, the gate stayed locked.

The forest glowed with vibrant colors as he stowed the key into his pocket, sunlight pouring down like it was late afternoon. He followed the worn path he'd traveled countless times. Though he'd memorized the way to the cabin, he still glanced at the star pins embedded in the tree trunks as he passed.

His boots crunched along the path as birds chirped overhead, his thoughts drifting back to the new family now living in his childhood home.

Who were they? Where had they come from?

Sadness stirred within him as the light breeze brushed through his dirty-blond hair. He'd always dreamed of one day buying back his family's property. Now it wouldn't be an option. He was curious about the newcomers, but he had no interest in meeting them.

Without warning, an image slammed into his mind. He closed his eyes, and the scene unfolded with vivid clarity.

Henry Snow stood in the kitchen, humming softly as he set out ingredients across the island. He pulled out a cutting board and knives, moving with calm certainty.

Henry was waiting for him.

He knew Caleb was on the way. Like always.

Caleb drew in a sharp breath as the forest shifted back into place around him. The vision faded as quickly as it came.

He took a few steadying breaths as he started walking again. The visions always caught him off guard.

They'd started after he first entered this realm—random flashes that came out of nowhere. Some felt like warnings. Others felt like glimpses of what was still to come. He wasn't sure why he got them, only that they'd helped him more than once.

The colorful trees gave way, and the cabin came into view. Smoke drifted lazily from the chimney, curling into the autumn sky.

Caleb grinned as he moved toward it. He walked straight to the door and stepped inside without knocking. The fire's heat wrapped around him at once, the scent of burning birch wood filling the cabin and easing the tightness in his chest.

Caleb exhaled slowly. He was home.

Henry stood at the kitchen island in a pristine button-down, sleeves rolled up. He was preparing to cook, just as Caleb had seen earlier.

"Perfect timing," Henry said, already moving toward him. He smiled, the wrinkles around his eyes deepening as he pulled Caleb into a quick hug. Caleb had grown taller and broader than the boy who'd first stumbled into the cabin, but Henry's warm embrace hadn't changed.

"What are we making today?" Caleb asked as he hung up his jacket.

"Fettuccine alfredo with fresh bread," Henry said, his voice chipper as he headed back to the kitchen.

"Sounds good to me." Caleb followed him, rolling up his sleeves.

They fell into an easy rhythm beside each other, moving around the kitchen without needing to say much. Cooking together had become a habit, something they did often.

"I think someone bought my old home," Caleb said as he stirred the sauce.

"They did," Henry said, continuing his work. After a brief pause, he added, "Would you like me to tell you about them?"

Caleb's fingers curled around the spoon as he swallowed back the rising emotion. Knowing would only make it worse. "No."

"Very well." Henry patted his shoulder as he went to set the table. "Let me know if you change your mind."

Caleb nodded, forcing back tears as he focused on the sauce.

Maybe one day he'd meet them. But for now, he'd keep his distance.

Chapter Twelve

"Henry and I made the best meals," Caleb said, sorrow coating his gaze as he stared into the kitchen.

Adeline smiled softly. She could easily picture Henry beside Caleb, happily teaching him the art of cooking. Henry had always loved to cook, but she had a feeling those times with Caleb mattered deeply to him. The thought only made her care for the old man more.

"I believe it," Adeline said. "I love his cooking."

Caleb didn't respond. He kept looking ahead, his jaw tightening as if he were still there with Henry. He had cared about him. She'd heard it in his voice and could see it now.

What had happened between them? Henry was the sweetest old man she'd ever known. What could have caused Caleb to despise him so much?

"I'm surprised my family and I never caught you sneaking across my backyard," Adeline said.

"I started going at night after your family moved in," he said, wincing as he readjusted on the couch. "I snuck out a lot."

"You weren't afraid Richard would catch you?"

Caleb gave a short, humorless huff. "Richard drank a lot. Once he passed out, he was out cold."

"Did things with him ever get better?"

"He still yelled," he said flatly, "but he stopped hitting me after I got bigger."

Adeline's eyes drifted over his thin frame. He looked fragile now. Nothing like the strong, athletic guy he must have been back then.

She let the silence settle before changing the subject. "What happened with Molly?"

"We started dating shortly after that," he said. "We were still together when I got stuck here."

"You two were together for a while."

"Yeah," he said after a moment. "She was a sweet girl."

Adeline couldn't help but imagine Molly: her smile, her laugh, the way she might have fit into Caleb's life back then. Whoever she was, she'd been important to him. That much was clear. "How did you get trapped in the Dark Territory?"

A shadow crossed his expression. He didn't answer right away. "I was an idiot."

"Did he capture you?"

A beat passed before he answered. "No."

"Then what happened?"

Caleb exhaled a long, slow breath as he leaned back into the couch and closed his only working eye. "I ran into someone in the forest."

***

Caleb stepped out of the cabin with a grin, a football tucked under his arm. Jesse lingered on the porch swing with a glass of water in hand, sweat trickling down his brow. They'd been throwing the ball around for over an hour.

Caleb tossed the football back to Jesse and lifted a hand. "See you later."

"Bye," Jesse called. "I'll go easy on you next time."

Caleb laughed, shaking his head as he stepped into the forest.

Senior year had begun, and things with Molly were good. Life was great. And for once, he believed it would stay that way.

He moved beneath a ceiling of green leaves, sunlight warming his skin. The fresh air felt more like spring than early fall as he thought back on his last visit with his friends. He'd spent the past few days with them and enjoyed every minute of it.

His mind came to a sudden halt as a strange sensation prickled along his spine. The hairs on the back of his neck rose as he slowed and reached for his hunting knife. He held it out before him, scanning the vivid forest around him. Everything looked peaceful, but the feeling wouldn't lift. He wasn't alone.

His senses snapped into focus. He'd walked this path countless times and had never run into anything dangerous, but that didn't mean it was safe. Having trained with Jesse, he was confident he could defend himself against whatever emerged.

"Caleb," a familiar voice whispered through the trees.

He froze.

He recognized that voice.

But it wasn't possible.

Caleb's heart pounded wildly as he spun, his eyes darting from tree to tree. "Grandpa?"

Leaves rustled behind him.

He whipped around, his breath catching as disbelief crashed over him. Stepping out from between two wide trunks was his grandfather—healthy, strong, and smiling. Not frail. Not pale. He looked exactly as Caleb remembered him before he got sick.

Grandpa wore khakis and a lightweight shirt, his smile warm as he strolled closer. "Hello, Little Wilder," he said, opening his arms.

Caleb sheathed the knife in one quick motion. "Is it really you?"

"It's really me."

Something inside Caleb broke open. He surged forward and pulled his grandfather into a tight embrace, holding on like he'd vanish if Caleb let go. A strangled laugh escaped him. Then the tears came, soaking Grandpa's shirt.

Grandpa. Here. In the forest.

Caleb stepped back, wiping his wet cheeks. "I've missed you."

"As I have missed you," Grandpa said, looking him over with pure pride. "My...look at you. You've grown up."

Caleb laughed through a sniffle. "I gained a little weight."

"Just a little?" Grandpa chuckled, his green eyes sparkling. "You look fantastic, my boy."

Caleb smiled. "I found the box you hid for me."

Grandpa's white brows lifted, and his face lit with delight. "Wonderful."

Caleb pulled the golden pocket watch from his pocket. "I carry this, and your note, everywhere I go." He flipped it open, revealing the folded paper tucked inside. "If it hadn't been for that note, I never would've found this world."

Grandpa reached out and squeezed Caleb's shoulder. "That's exactly why I left it."

Joy rushed through Caleb as he closed the watch and slipped it back into his pocket. "How is this happening? Do you live in this world now?"

Grandpa nodded, his smile pleasant. "I've been here for quite some time."

"Really?" Caleb's brows rose. "I had no idea."

Grandpa's expression dimmed. "I've tried numerous times to reach out to you. But that large, redheaded man at that cabin wouldn't allow it."

"Are you talking about Godfrey?" he asked, confusion tightening his chest.

"Yes," Grandpa said with a slow nod.

"That doesn't sound like something he would do."

"And that," Grandpa said, lifting a single finger, "is where you're wrong. He may seem genuine, but I assure you—it is all an act."

Caleb studied his wrinkly face. "But Grandpa...I thought you were friends with him."

"Ha!" Grandpa released a sharp laugh. "Is that what he told you?"

"Yeah."

"Silly boy," he said, shaking his head. "You weren't always this gullible."

A war raged inside Caleb as years of memories at the cabin flashed through his mind—shared meals, laughter, games. None of it felt fake. "But they're my friends. They've never done anything wrong to me."

Grandpa tilted his head. "Would true friends keep you from your family?"

Caleb faltered. "No...but—"

"They're the ones who have kept us apart." Sternness washed over Grandpa's aged face as he leaned closer. "Take my advice and stay away from them. They are not what they seem."

Unease rolled through Caleb as he shifted his weight, struggling to make sense of his grandfather's words. He'd trusted his friends. Cared about them. Never once had he believed they were hiding something so dark.

And yet...

Why hadn't they told him about Grandpa?

"I must go, Little Wilder," Grandpa said, reluctance threading his tone. "I'll see you again soon."

"Please don't leave." Caleb gripped his thin arm.

"There's urgent business I must attend to," Grandpa said, easing Caleb's hand away, "but I promise, we will meet again."

"How will I find you?"

"I live in a beautiful territory not far from here." Grandpa gestured through the trees. "Keep walking that way until you reach the cliff that overlooks a field of wild poppies. Then pass through the thick tree line beyond it."

Caleb went still. "Wait...are you talking about the Dark Territory?"

"Yes. A strange name for such a spectacular place." Grandpa chuckled softly. "Have you ever been inside it?"

"Well...no."

"There is nothing dark about it. It's quite stunning."

Caleb searched his green eyes, desperately wanting to believe him. "I've been told not to go in there because it's dangerous."

Grandpa scoffed. "Your *friends* told you that?"

Caleb scuffed his shoe through the dirt, his gaze dropping to the ground. "Yeah."

"Don't you see?" Grandpa placed his frail hand back on Caleb's broad shoulder. "They want to keep you from me. They want you all to themselves."

"But why? We could all hang out together."

"They'd never allow that," he said, giving Caleb's shoulder a gentle, affection-ate squeeze before stepping back. "Will you come visit me soon?"

Caleb wrestled with the idea, but only for a second. He'd do anything to see his grandfather again. "I will."

"Good." Grandpa smiled once more. "I'll see you later."

He gave Caleb a final wave before disappearing behind a large tree, its thick leaves rustling softly. Caleb remained where he was, staring at the empty space long after his grandfather was gone.

Nothing about this made sense. His grandfather had never lied to him. Not once. And the idea that his so-called friends had kept something this important from him made his chest tighten.

Betrayal and hurt settled deep as Caleb started his walk back toward his old backyard.

If they lied to me about the Dark Territory...about Grandpa...

What else have they lied about?

They were his friends. Or at least, he'd thought they were.

He'd been warned never to set foot in Ralock's land.

But the next time he visited, he would.

Caleb wanted to see his grandfather again, and if the only way to do that was to enter that forbidden place, so be it.

Chapter Thirteen

It didn't take Caleb long to find the Dark Territory the next day. He knew exactly where it was. He'd seen it from a distance more than once while exploring the forest.

An uneasy feeling urged him to turn back, but he kept walking. He followed the narrow path beside the cliff and stepped into a field of bright-red poppy flowers, their delicate petals brushing against his legs. The blooms stretched out before him like a sea of red, swaying gently in the warm breeze as he made his way toward the thick tree line beyond.

The forest on the other side looked almost identical to the one Caleb had always roamed. It was lush and green beneath the brilliant sun. Evergreens and leafy trees covered a mountain range that dominated the horizon.

It was breathtaking.

And yet, a warning prickled along his spine as he crossed into the territory. The land was bright and full of life. Nothing about it looked dangerous. But something felt...off.

He shook it away and focused on the beauty around him. Ferns blanketed the forest floor beneath towering trunks whose branches wove together high above. Moss-covered rocks peeked through the greenery like ancient stones half-claimed by the earth.

I can't believe they lied to me about this place.

A well-trodden path came into view, and Caleb eagerly followed it. Vibrant green leaves rustled overhead as sunlight filtered through the canopy. He breathed in the fresh air and took his time, letting the trail lead him deeper into the territory.

Snap!

Caleb jumped back, his heart slamming against his ribs as he grabbed his hunting knife.

"Who's there?" he said, holding the blade out in front of him.

No one answered.

"Show yourself!"

There was a faint rustle ahead of him.

A thin girl emerged from the trees, her tattered dress hanging loosely from her narrow frame. Dark hair clung to her face, and her bare feet moved silently across the forest floor. She looked about his age, but the fear in her eyes made her look older.

"Who are you?" she asked, caution in her tone.

Caleb steadied his breathing and lowered his knife. "I'm Caleb."

She looked him over, narrowing her gaze on his bare forearm. She glanced left, then right, as if expecting someone to appear. Stepping closer, she lowered her voice to a whisper. "Leave while you still can."

A sudden snap of a twig sent her bolting into the trees.

"Wait!" Caleb called, taking off after her.

Branches cracked beneath him as he chased her, but she moved with startling speed. Within seconds, she vanished behind the thick veil of green leaves, leaving no trace behind.

Caleb slowed to a walk, his chest burning.

Why would she tell me to leave?

Was it a trick? Or a warning he should take seriously?

A blood-curdling scream ripped through the forest.

Caleb froze. It was close.

Gripping his knife tightly, he pushed forward, following the fading cries until he found her.

The girl lay crumpled on the ground, her tiny frame curled into a ball. Blood soaked through her dress, dark against the pale fabric. A small knife was buried in her side.

Caleb's heart dropped. He spun in a slow circle, searching for danger, before rushing to her side and kneeling down. She was gasping for air, her breath shallow and uneven, her wide eyes pinned to his.

"Run," she mouthed, barely audible.

Before Caleb could respond, her eyes went still and her body went limp.

Footsteps pounded behind him.

Caleb sprang to his feet, panic surging through him. He didn't stop to look—he ran. Branches whipped at his arms and roots clawed at his feet as he tore through the forest. His lungs burned and his thoughts raced.

The girl's final word echoed in his head.

Run.

He skidded to a stop when a figure stepped onto the path ahead.

"Little Wilder," Grandpa said with a wide smile. "I see you've found me after all."

Caleb stared at him, his breath coming in ragged bursts as his grip stayed firm around the knife in his hand. Relief and confusion collided in his chest as he struggled to make sense of how his grandfather had found him there. He glanced back over his shoulder, half-expecting to hear the footsteps again, but the forest stood silent behind him.

"What's wrong?" Grandpa asked, his wrinkled face stitched with concern.

"There was a girl," Caleb said between breaths. "Someone killed her."

Grandpa's expression sobered. "Show me."

Caleb hesitated. Every instinct screamed at him to leave, to put as much distance between himself and that place as possible, but he wanted his grandfather to see. "Okay," he said, his breathing still heavy.

They retraced Caleb's steps, the trees seeming to close in tighter the farther they went. When they reached the spot, Caleb stopped short.

The girl was gone.

His stomach twisted as he looked at the lone bloodstain darkening the ground. *Where did she go? Who took her?*

Grandpa crouched, studying the earth. "Probably an animal," he said, straightening. "They don't always leave much behind."

Caleb swallowed while staring at the dark stain at his feet. "There was a knife," he said, the words catching in his throat. "Stuck in her side."

Grandpa paused. For a fraction of a second, something unreadable crossed his face before he smoothed it away. He gave Caleb a sympathetic grin. "This land plays tricks on people. Especially when you're frightened."

Caleb kept looking at the blood as unease gripped him. He knew what he had seen. Or at least, he thought he did.

The girl's warning rang in his mind, louder this time.

Run.

But it seemed like nonsense now that he was with Grandpa. He had nothing to fear. Whatever or whoever had harmed that girl was long gone by now.

"Come on," Grandpa said warmly. "Let's forget about that unfortunate girl and let me show you around." He placed a firm hand on Caleb's back and urged him forward. "You're safe with me."

As Caleb let himself be guided away, the forest seemed to press in behind them. Only the leaves stirred, whispering softly in the breeze. He didn't look back, not at the bloodstain or the place where the girl had fallen.

He shook his head, pushing the image from his mind. He was with his grandfather now, and that was all he chose to focus on.

Chapter Fourteen

With Grandpa beside him, the Dark Territory no longer felt threatening. Evergreens stood along the winding paths, tucked between broad oaks and hickories. Pine needles cushioned their steps, releasing a faint earthy scent as they walked. They spent the next few hours wandering through the woods, the tension of earlier fading with each passing moment.

Being with Grandpa felt unreal, like a dream Caleb hadn't expected to come true. He never imagined he would see him again, especially in this strange world he'd grown to love.

Sunlight streamed between the branches in soft, golden streaks as they talked and reminisced. Caleb filled Grandpa in on how much his life had changed over the past few years: football, Molly, his foster family. There was much to catch him up on.

Grandpa listened as he always had. He smiled and nodded with genuine interest. He never interrupted, as though he'd been waiting to hear every word.

Time slipped by unnoticed as the day wore on. The Dark Territory twisted and branched in every direction, its trails just as confusing as the forest he knew, and Caleb quickly lost any sense of where they were. It felt like a maze, but he didn't mind.

Strangely, Caleb hadn't thought about his friends back at the cabin since he had arrived. That surprised him. They had become his family, always lingering at the edge of his thoughts.

But here, with Grandpa, nothing else mattered.

Crunch! Crunch! Crunch!

The sound of boots tearing through the forest erupted out of nowhere, growing louder by the second.

Caleb tensed, stepping closer to Grandpa.

A man in black tactical gear emerged from the trees and jogged straight toward them, a sheathed knife at his hip.

Grandpa didn't flinch. "Don't be alarmed," he said, raising a hand. "He's a friend."

The military man slowed as he approached. He was about the same height as Caleb, with a powerful build. Thick black armor covered his body, heavy enough to stop a bullet, and his dark brown eyes held a fierce intensity that made Caleb cringe.

The man stopped in front of Grandpa, placed his right fist against his chest, and bowed his head. "Master. I've been looking everywhere for you."

Master? Caleb's face scrunched. *Why'd he call Grandpa that?*

"Well." Grandpa squared his shoulders, his posture suddenly rigid. "You've found me. This is my grandson, Caleb."

A chill slid down Caleb's spine as the man's eyes traveled over him, cold and unimpressed. "Grandson?"

"Do you have a problem with that?" Grandpa asked, his expression darkening.

The man immediately lowered his eyes. "No, sir."

"Good," Grandpa said. "Now, what do you want?"

"He escaped." He stepped closer, his words barely above a whisper.

Grandpa stiffened, the muscles in his jaw flexing. "What?"

Despite the man's size and armor, fear flashed across his face as he took an involuntary step back. Grandpa closed the distance between them, pressing a finger into the center of the man's armored chest as he spoke in a low, controlled tone.

Caleb watched in silence, startled by a side of his grandfather he'd never seen before. The man he'd grown up with had always been gentle and soft-spoken, never raising his voice or confronting anyone...until now.

He couldn't hear what Grandpa was saying, but whatever it was made the armored man tense. It made no sense. Grandpa was smaller, older, and unarmed. Yet the soldier was clearly afraid.

Grandpa shoved him back.

The man gave Caleb a quick glance before turning and vanishing into the trees.

"I'm sorry you had to see that." Grandpa smoothed down his shirt and smiled over at Caleb as if nothing had happened. "I've learned that you must be firm with the people who live here."

"Who was that?" Caleb asked.

"He's a warrior," Grandpa said, his white hair lifting faintly in the breeze. "Part of the military."

Caleb frowned. "I didn't realize this place had a military."

"Oh, yes." Grandpa nodded. "It is vital to keep our borders secure." He paused, and a knowing look crossed his face. "I take it you didn't notice him."

He pointed up into the trees, and Caleb followed his gaze. It took him a second, but once he saw it, he couldn't unsee it.

A small platform resembling a hunting stand was strapped high against a thick tree. A man stood within it, perfectly still, a solid black bow drawn loosely at his side. His face was painted in heavy camouflage, blending so completely into the surroundings that Caleb couldn't tell where the man ended and the forest began.

His breath hitched.

The man hadn't moved. He hadn't shifted. He hadn't even blinked.

When their eyes met, the air left Caleb's lungs.

They were yellow.

Fear crept through Caleb's veins. Everything in him urged him to flee, but his legs wouldn't move.

"He's one of our hunters," Grandpa said plainly. "That's the other branch of the military."

"I didn't even see him," Caleb whispered, his hands trembling at his sides.

"That's the point," Grandpa said, tipping his chin toward the trees. "Our hunters and watchtowers are designed to blend in."

High above them, the hunter acknowledged Grandpa with a brief nod, his dark green armor blending seamlessly with the forest. "Master."

Grandpa returned the nod, and the hunter looked away, resuming his watch.

Unease coiled in Caleb as he looked at his grandfather. Soft green eyes met his, framed by deep wrinkles and sun-spotted skin. It was the same face he'd known all his life, but something in his stare was unfamiliar.

He pushed the thought away, convincing himself it was nothing. "Why did he call you master?"

Grandpa chuckled. "I thought you might ask." He folded his hands behind his back, his tone easy, almost amused. "I suppose it does sound strange, but I am one of the leaders of this territory. Second in command."

Caleb stood there, letting the words settle.

"I work closely with Ralock."

Caleb blinked at him, his mouth suddenly going dry. "Ralock?"

The name made his skin crawl. He'd never met Ralock, but his friends had warned him about that monster and the things he'd done. But what if that was a lie too? Surely his grandfather wouldn't align himself with someone dangerous.

"Yes," Grandpa said, nodding. "He rules over this entire region and has asked for my help."

Caleb felt the blood drain from his face. This had to be a misunderstanding. It had to be.

"I've already spoken to him about you," Grandpa continued. "He has no objections to me training you—to prepare you to become a leader as well."

"But Grandpa..." His voice wavered despite his effort to steady it. "I've heard terrible things about Ralock."

"I'm sure you have," Grandpa said, irritation crossing his face. "Your so-called friends are quite good at making up stories."

"But why would they do that?"

Grandpa shrugged. "To scare you. To keep you away from power—real power—that can only come from Ralock."

Caleb's thoughts scrambled. He'd spent so much time with Godfrey, Henry, and Jesse, never once questioning their intentions. And yet, standing here now, his grandfather's words landed in a way that made doubt creep in, followed by resentment.

"So, what do you say?" Grandpa asked. "Will you join us?"

Caleb ran a hand through his hair, studying his grandfather's face. He'd never cared about power before, but the way Grandpa spoke about it pulled at something deep inside him. Something he couldn't ignore.

"I'll do it," he said.

"Excellent!" Grandpa clapped his hands. "I have other matters that need my attention right now. But next time you visit, we can begin your first lesson."

"Okay."

"This way," Grandpa said, turning around. "I'll drop you off at the poppy field."

Excitement mixed with unease wrestled within Caleb as they made their way back toward the entrance. A gentle breeze drifted between the trees, lifting the edge of his shirt. It didn't make sense. He was finally reunited with his grandfather. This was what he wanted.

And yet the feeling refused to leave.

When they finally reached the meadow, Caleb stepped into the flowers and turned back. "Bye, Grandpa."

"Goodbye, Little Wilder," he said, lifting a hand. "I'll see you soon."

Caleb parted the poppies and climbed the steep path toward the forest. He took the trail that would return him to his world, nowhere near the cabin.

Anger followed him with every step. He couldn't believe they'd lied to him—about Grandpa, about Ralock, about everything.

Still, the thought of leading a territory alongside his grandfather sparked something warm and thrilling inside him.

I wonder what it's going to be like.

As Caleb's thoughts drifted back to the idea of becoming a leader, the sound of footfalls drew him out of it. He turned just as Jesse stepped into view.

"Sorry, Caleb." Jesse gave a crooked smile, one hand resting on the hilt of his sword. "Didn't mean to scare you."

"Hey, Jesse."

"Heading home already?"

"Yeah."

"I see." Jesse's smile faded, replaced by something more serious. "I'll walk you back."

It was the last thing Caleb wanted, but he didn't object.

They started down the trail together. Jesse walked beside him. Sticks crunched beneath their shoes, the sound loud in the silence. Caleb's muscles stayed tight, his mind racing. He couldn't wait to get away from Jesse.

"Caleb," Jesse said at last, his voice calm but firm. "Why do you think we warn you about exploring certain territories on your own?"

Heat crept up Caleb's neck as his lips pressed tight. He refused to look at Jesse as they walked.

"It's for your safety," Jesse continued when he didn't answer. "We want you to explore. To enjoy this world. But it isn't like yours."

"I know that, Jesse!" Caleb snapped, his words sharper than he intended. "I've been coming here for years."

Jesse didn't flinch at Caleb's outburst. He stopped walking and turned to face him, his expression calm and controlled. "Caleb, the Dark Territory is dangerous. You cannot go back there."

Anger surged through Caleb as he clenched his fists. He was done being told what he could and couldn't do. "You're just trying to keep me away from my grandfather."

Jesse's jaw tightened, just slightly. "That's not true. I would never do that to you."

"Then why didn't you tell me he was alive?" Caleb demanded. "Why didn't you tell me he was here?"

Concern creased Jesse's brow. "You think I'd keep something like that from you?"

"That doesn't answer my question," Caleb said through clenched teeth. "I trusted you. I thought you were family. But I was wrong."

He turned away, but Jesse caught his arm.

"Caleb, wait."

Caleb yanked free. "Leave me alone."

He stormed down the trail without looking back.

The trees blurred as fury clouded his vision. The anger stayed with him, but beneath it was something worse. Hurt. Disappointment. He'd trusted them. Cared about them.

At least he had his grandfather now. He didn't have to waste his time at the cabin anymore.

Caleb didn't slow until the gate came into view. Beyond it, his old backyard lay dark and still, like a photograph frozen in time.

He stared at it briefly, then looked away. Only then did he stop and let out a long breath, his chest tight with emotions he didn't want to name.

He told himself he'd made the right choice. That trusting his grandfather made sense. He'd raised Caleb, after all.

And for now, that was all he needed.

Chapter Fifteen

"Whoa." Caleb turned in a circle, taking in the vast city around him. "You live here?"

"I sure do." Grandpa's wrinkles deepened as he smiled.

It was Caleb's second day in the Dark Territory, and Grandpa had decided to show him around the only city in the heart of the region. Caleb stood in the city square, which was easily three times the size of the small town he'd grown up in.

People moved in every direction, voices overlapping and footsteps echoing against the stone. The place felt electric, busy in a way he hadn't expected. Until now, he'd only known the cabin, garden, and forest. Seeing a city here, one that operated so much like his own world, left him speechless.

The sunlight touched his face as a cold breeze brushed against him, tugging at his long-sleeved shirt. The air carried a slight stench, but it barely registered over the rush of excitement. Shops lined the street, stretching as far as he could see. Doors swung open and shut as people moved in and out.

There were supermarkets and bakeries, hardware stores and restaurants. Even a library. An antique shop rose three stories high, its windows packed with forgotten things.

Caleb couldn't stop staring.

They moved with the flow of people along the cobblestones. There were no vehicles, only the warriors who patrolled the city on horseback. They rode through the crowd, their presence cold and commanding.

Caleb held his breath as he hurried past one, eyeing the black sword strapped to his hip. Grandpa had made him leave his hunting knife behind in the poppy field. Only the military was permitted to carry weapons in the territory. He'd told Caleb not to worry, but the warriors still made him nervous.

The city fascinated him more the farther they walked. The size. The movement. The possibilities. Knowing he might one day rule over it only heightened his excitement.

Then the crowd shifted, and the gallows came into view. The wide wooden platform rose above the square, weathered and darkened with age. Its beams were scarred by years of use.

Caleb stopped short. It wasn't the structure that made his stomach drop; it was the body hanging from one of the nooses.

Queasiness churned as he stared up at the decaying corpse swaying gently in the breeze. He wanted to look away, but he couldn't.

A crow landed on the beam above the body, its black eyes scanning the square below. Another joined it. Then a third.

Caleb shuddered.

Grandpa leaned closer. "Our justice system is a little bit different here."

"What did he do?"

"He set his neighbor's house on fire," Grandpa said. "Killed all three people inside."

"That's terrible," Caleb said, dropping his gaze.

"It is. Which is why we take extreme measures to ensure it doesn't happen again."

Caleb wasn't sure he agreed with hanging criminals, but he kept the thought to himself. As he glanced around, something else caught his attention.

Iron bars. Every window and every door had them.

The city suddenly felt less like a city and more like a prison.

"Why are there bars on everything?"

"For protection," Grandpa said, raising a hand to shade his eyes from the sun.

"From what?"

"There's a large homeless population. Some of them steal."

Caleb glanced toward the gallows. "Do they get hanged for that too?"

Grandpa laughed softly. "Of course not. The gallows are reserved for serious crimes."

A stranger collided with Caleb's shoulder, sending him stumbling a step. He steadied himself and watched as the man disappeared into the crowd without a glance back.

The crowd closed in around him.

People of every nationality and age hurried past, but something odd stood out to him. There were no children. Everyone looked older than thirteen, their faces tight with anger or worn down by exhaustion. It was nothing like Black Mountain, where smiles came easily and people acknowledged one another as they passed.

Most wore ordinary clothes, but the homeless were impossible to miss. Dressed in dirty rags, they dug through bins or crouched along the street begging for money.

"Why are there so many homeless people?" Caleb asked, watching them carefully.

"Laziness," Grandpa replied, casting a brief look toward a homeless man. "There are plenty of jobs available. Not everyone is willing to work."

Caleb said nothing. He looked at the hollow faces of those begging for help, wishing he could do something.

"Let's get some breakfast," Grandpa suggested.

Caleb stayed close to his grandfather as he followed him toward the line of stores. He was bumped into more than once, the people rushing past him without apologizing.

Irritation had set in by the time they reached the curb. The diner they stepped into was outdated and cramped. Metal chairs clashed with shabby booths, and the stained floor looked like it hadn't been cleaned in years. A faint smell of mold clung to the air, mingling with the odor of fried food.

Nothing about the diner was appealing. It reminded Caleb of a hole-in-the-wall restaurant that only locals would tolerate. Under normal circumstances, he would never eat in a place like this. But he kept his mouth shut and followed Grandpa to the counter.

"What are you having?" the overweight woman asked. She eyed them with annoyance, her gray hair pulled back so tightly it looked painful.

Caleb forced a polite smile as Grandpa stepped forward.

"Two blueberry bagels," Grandpa said. "Loaded with cream cheese."

She gave them a hard look, wiping her hands on her apron. "Four coins."

Grandpa reached into his pocket and dropped four copper coins onto the counter.

The woman scooped them up, counted them quickly, then looked back at him. "The tattoo."

Grandpa pushed up his sleeve, revealing a black cobra coiled around his forearm.

The cashier gave it a quick glance before turning away to prepare their order.

Caleb studied the black ink. Grandpa had always disliked tattoos. Why did he have one now?

"I thought you didn't like tattoos," Caleb said as they waited.

"I do now," Grandpa said, a hint of humor in his voice. "The only way to live in this territory is to become one of Ralock's followers. It's as simple as getting this tattoo."

Grandpa held out his arm, the skin wrinkled and thin with age. The black cobra was detailed and precise, the ink so lifelike it looked ready to strike.

Tattoos had never bothered Caleb, but this one did.

"Want to go ahead and get yours?" Grandpa lifted his white brows.

"No, thanks."

Grandpa rolled his sleeve back down. "You won't be able to do much here without it."

"What does that mean?"

"The only way you can buy or sell in this territory is to have Ralock's tattoo on your forearm."

Caleb frowned. "That's an odd requirement."

"It's just one of the rules," Grandpa said. "It keeps outsiders from showing up and disrupting our government."

"What if someone wants to live here but doesn't want that tattoo?" Caleb asked. "Are they forced to get it?"

Grandpa chuckled. "Of course not. No one is ever forced. Everyone chooses it freely." He paused, then added, "But Ralock won't allow anyone to reside here without it."

Caleb nodded slowly, though his shoulders remained tense. "That's...interesting."

"No need to worry. You can get it whenever you're ready."

The woman dropped a careless dab of cream cheese onto the bagels and shoved the tin plate toward Grandpa. The same black cobra was inked on her forearm.

A strange feeling settled over Caleb as he followed Grandpa to an empty booth. The vinyl seat clung to the back of his denim pants when he sat down.

Grandpa placed a napkin on his lap and grabbed his bagel.

Caleb did the same. But the moment he bit into the cold bagel, he nearly spat it out. It was stale and bland, easily the worst thing he'd ever tasted. He chewed anyway, not wanting to be rude.

"How is it?" Grandpa asked, smiling.

"It's good," Caleb lied.

Grandpa's smile widened as he took another bite. Caleb swallowed hard, the taste worsening. To distract himself, he glanced around the diner.

The place was packed, but no one looked content. Faces were tight and brows furrowed as raised voices dominated the space. Arguments outnumbered laughter, and the constant clatter of plates and chairs only added to the thick tension hanging in the air.

Caleb shifted in his seat. He'd never been in a public place that felt so hostile. He leaned across the table, lowering his voice. "Why does everyone seem so angry?"

Grandpa stifled a grin. "They aren't angry. They're just very blunt and expressive."

Caleb glanced at a nearby table where two women were arguing. "Looks like anger to me."

"This territory values directness," Grandpa said, using his napkin to wipe his mouth. "Strict rules. Clear expectations. There's no flattery or southern hospitality here. Just honest conversations that can sound harsh if you're not used to them."

Caleb stared down at his bagel, his appetite gone. The explanation made sense logically, and yet unease continued to stir in his gut, a quiet warning he couldn't quite shake.

He ignored it, blaming the stale food and sour atmosphere.

"You'll get used to it," Grandpa said confidently.

"I hope so."

"You'll find that this place is very similar to the world you come from."

Caleb raised an eyebrow. "You mean the world *we* come from."

"Yes, of course," he said, shaking his head lightly. "I sometimes forget. I've been here for so long."

Caleb watched his grandfather take another bite of his bagel. He looked exactly the same as Caleb remembered. His mannerisms. The way he sat and ate.

But something had changed. The warmth was gone, replaced by a rough seriousness that felt foreign. Leading the military must have done that to him.

"Finish your breakfast," Grandpa said. "Then I'll show you where I live."

Caleb glanced down at the remaining bagel and pushed it aside. "I'm done."

"Are you sure?"

"Yeah. I wasn't that hungry."

"All right, then." Grandpa stood. "Let's go."

***

Caleb stepped toward the massive glass window that made up an entire wall of his grandfather's penthouse. From this height, the city stretched for miles, nestled between the surrounding forest. Neighborhoods and towering buildings spread out below, the streets alive with movement.

"See anything interesting?" Grandpa called from behind him.

Caleb turned and nearly laughed.

His grandfather lounged in a yellow accent chair, his casual clothes clashing with the refined space.

"I didn't realize the city was so big," Caleb said as he lowered himself onto a stiff leather couch across from Grandpa. It was clearly designed more for style than for comfort.

He glanced around the room. The space was sleek and modern, every surface spotless as if no one truly lived there. The minimal décor looked expensive, nothing like the old, cluttered home they'd once shared.

He kept looking around until he realized his grandfather was studying him.

"Do you like my place?" Grandpa asked, gesturing to the tidy room.

Caleb shrugged, forcing a small smile. "It's different."

"I like different."

"I can see that." Caleb laughed.

Grandpa joined in, but the humor faded quickly, and his expression turned serious. "If you decide to become Ralock's follower, I can get you your own place," Grandpa said. "You can decorate it however you like."

Caleb sat up straight. "Really?"

"Of course." Enthusiasm lit his aged face. "I'm extremely wealthy here. I can buy whatever I want."

"That's so weird," Caleb said, lightly shaking his head. "We never had money when you were alive in our world."

"Well, I do now." Grandpa rose to his feet and crossed the room to the wet bar, where liquor bottles of every shape and color lined the shelves. He reached for the scotch and poured a generous amount into two glasses. He smiled as he returned, extending one toward Caleb. "Let's celebrate."

Caleb shifted uncomfortably in his seat. Since when did Grandpa drink alcohol?

A tight knot formed in his stomach as he watched the brown liquid swirl in the glass. The grandfather he'd grown up with had never touched alcohol and had strongly warned Caleb against it. So why was he drinking now? And why was he pressuring Caleb to join him?

"I'm only eighteen," he said, grasping for an excuse.

"Lucky for you," Grandpa said, nudging the glass closer, "there's no drinking age here."

Caleb stared at the glass. He didn't want it, but his grandfather was watching. Waiting. With a sigh, Caleb took the scotch, the strong smell stinging his nose.

"To new beginnings." Grandpa lifted his glass and drank.

Caleb raised the glass to his lips and took a careful sip. Bitterness burned his throat as he forced it down, fighting the urge to cough. He kept his expression neutral, pretending it didn't bother him.

A strange heat curled in his stomach.

He didn't like it, but he could still feel Grandpa's eyes on him.

So he took another sip.

Chapter Sixteen

The first week passed in a blur. Caleb spent nearly every hour with his grandfather, learning the structure of Ralock's territory and the power that ruled it. Grandpa was nothing like the man he remembered—stricter, harsher, commanding respect wherever he went.

Caleb admired it.

Even when he disagreed with Grandpa's methods, he stayed quiet and obeyed. Questioning authority wasn't tolerated in the Dark Territory. Besides, Caleb wanted what Grandpa had.

Power.

He stopped visiting the cabin altogether. Instead, he followed Grandpa through the city, the barracks, and the borders of the land. The territory was enormous. The woods stretched for miles, the mountain range split the land in two, and a single city stood at its center where everything happened.

And Ralock ruled it all.

Though Caleb hadn't met him yet, his presence lingered everywhere. In the laws. The weapons. The soldiers. Grandpa promised Caleb would meet him once he got the cobra tattoo.

Caleb avoided the subject. He was curious, but the thought never sat right with him. He didn't want a tattoo, especially not one of a snake.

The barracks were where he learned the most.

Hunters and warriors filled the space—hundreds of them. Their weapons were black-bladed and infused with Ralock's power, transforming ordinary fighters into unstoppable forces.

All the hunters were identical, clones created by Ralock's scientists, while the warriors were followers that Ralock had personally recruited and trained himself.

Caleb watched them patrol the city, enforce the law, and kill anyone who resisted.

Fear became normal.

Despite the violence, Caleb found the Dark Territory fascinating. Grandpa told him he needed to be tougher if he wanted to survive there. Caleb believed him. He wanted to stay. He wanted to belong.

But ultimately, he wanted to help rule.

***

"Sorry to interrupt," said the hunter named Cutler as he stepped into the dim library.

Grandpa and Caleb watched him approach. Hatred hardened Cutler's camouflaged face, and the sight of him made Caleb cringe.

Cutler was easy to distinguish from the rest of the hunters. Caleb wasn't sure how the tip of his nose had been sliced off, or how he'd earned the long scar running up the left side of his face, but one thing was certain.

He was terrifying.

"What is it?" Grandpa asked, remaining seated as he glanced up at the hunter.

Cutler leaned down and whispered into Grandpa's ear. Caleb couldn't hear the words, but he didn't need to. Grandpa's jaw flexed. The veins in his neck pulsed as he sprang up and replied sharply in a language Caleb didn't recognize.

He'd never heard that dialect before, and he had no memory of his grandfather being bilingual.

Just as suddenly, Grandpa switched back to his normal tone. "Go get him."

Cutler gave a slight bow.

"I want to go with you." Caleb stood.

"No," Cutler growled, his yellow eyes narrowing.

"Why not?"

"You're *not* a hunter."

"Now, now," Grandpa said, stepping smoothly between them. "There's no need to get upset."

Cutler gave Grandpa a tense look before leaning in and speaking in a hushed tone. They murmured back and forth, their voices too low for Caleb to catch. The only words he heard clearly were Grandpa's.

"I need him."

A cold ripple moved through Caleb. He knew Grandpa was talking about him, and though he didn't understand what it meant, the tone alone made his skin crawl. He tucked the feeling away when Grandpa turned and grinned at him.

"Of course you can go, my boy," Grandpa said, gripping Cutler's shoulder and giving it a quick shake. "Cutler would love for you to tag along."

One look at the hunter told Caleb that it was a lie. Cutler's thin, painted lips pressed into a tight line, and his narrowing gaze made Caleb's blood run cold.

Still, Caleb held his ground. "Great," he said. "I'm ready when you are."

Cutler shot Grandpa one last cold stare before turning toward the doorway and striding out of the room.

"You'd better get going." Grandpa sat back on the couch, looking satisfied. "He isn't going to wait for you."

Caleb hurried after him, catching up just as Cutler rounded the corner. Cutler didn't spare him a glance. He moved fast down the corridor, his combat boots pounding against the floor.

They burst through the front doors, and the cold air bit into Caleb's face.

Cutler didn't slow. He bounded down the steps, his boots striking the cobblestone as he pulled a small device from his pocket and glanced at it. As he moved, people along the street quickly stepped aside, parting without a word.

Caleb followed close behind, studying the circular object in the hunter's hand. At first, it looked like a compass, but there was a blinking red dot on the glass screen. It shifted as Cutler moved.

"What is that?" Caleb called out.

Cutler ignored him, his eyes fixed on the device as he veered toward the woods.

"Hello?" Caleb pressed. "I know you can hear me."

Cutler stopped. He drew a slow breath before turning around. His snake-like eyes locked onto Caleb.

Caleb stepped back. Cutler wasn't much bigger than him, but the leather armor made him feel larger and more dangerous.

"Just because you were allowed to come," Cutler said coldly, "doesn't mean you can speak."

Caleb stiffened.

"The man we're tracking is dangerous," Cutler continued. "I won't have you distracting me."

"I wasn't distracting you." Caleb didn't break eye contact. His heart raced, but he kept his face calm, just like Grandpa had taught him. "I just asked what you're using."

Cutler cast him a cynical look before turning back to the screen. "It's my map."

"And the flashing dot?" Caleb nodded toward it.

"Our target."

"How does it—"

"Our technology is advanced," Cutler interrupted. "Enough questions. We need to move before he escapes."

Caleb had a dozen more questions about the technology—how it worked, who built it, what else it could do—but he kept them to himself and followed Cutler into the woods.

The red dot on the digital map crept closer with every step. Branches snagged at Caleb's sleeves and thorns scraped against his pant legs as he pushed deeper into the undergrowth alongside Cutler. Brittle twigs snapped beneath their boots, the sound carrying farther than Caleb liked.

After nearly a quarter mile, Cutler reached for the sheath at his side and drew a short sword with a black blade. Caleb tensed at the sight. He still wasn't used to those creepy weapons.

A cold wind whispered through the leaves as they came to a stop. They were practically on top of the red dot. Cutler slipped the device back into his pocket and pressed himself against a thick tree. Caleb mirrored him, crouching low as adrenaline sharpened his senses.

The woods fell unnaturally quiet. The leaves stilled. Even the insects went silent, leaving only the sound of Caleb's breathing in his ears.

Then a branch cracked nearby.

"Don't move," Cutler whispered.

Caleb went still as Cutler stepped away from the tree and moved toward the sound. He blended into the forest so seamlessly that Caleb nearly lost sight of him, as if he had dissolved into the trees.

Holding his breath, Caleb strained to see who would emerge.

A tall, slender man came into view.

He limped forward, clutching his blood-soaked side. His clothes hung in rags, and he looked no different from the homeless men Caleb had seen wandering the streets. Unarmed. Weak. Harmless.

Or so Caleb thought.

"Hello there," Cutler said, a mocking edge in his voice. "I've been expecting you."

The man went pale. His body trembled as his gaze dropped to the blade in Cutler's hand. "Please," he stammered, shuffling backward. "I didn't mean to hurt her."

"Oh, but you did." Cutler strode toward him.

The man whimpered, pressing his bloodied hand harder against his side as he tried to retreat. But there was nowhere to go.

Cutler struck. His blade plunged into the man's gut, and a scream tore through the woods as he stabbed again and again.

Caleb stood rooted to the spot, horror locking his limbs in place. His ears rang. The forest tilted. The screams wouldn't stop.

He turned away, his breath sharp and uneven as panic clawed up his throat.

Finally, the sounds stopped.

Silence followed.

When Caleb looked back, Cutler was wiping the blood from his blade onto his dark green tactical pants.

Caleb pressed a hand against the trunk beside him, steadying himself. He had just witnessed a murder.

"What's the matter, boy?" Cutler sneered. "Scared of a little blood?"

Caleb pushed away from the tree and straightened, hiding his shaky hands in his pockets. "I thought you were going to arrest him."

"There's no tolerance for murder here." Cutler sheathed the blade. "Especially within our military."

"He didn't look dangerous," Caleb said, keeping his eyes off the body.

Cutler smirked. "Looks deceive. He killed one of our warriors with a butcher knife this morning."

Caleb swallowed, bile burning at the back of his throat. They left the body behind without a word. He couldn't stop seeing the blade. Hearing the screams.

He pressed his lips together, fighting the urge to double over as he forced his trembling legs to keep moving.

When they returned to the barracks, his thoughts were scattered. The image replayed in his mind, refusing to fade, but his face remained blank.

If he wanted to help rule here, he would have to get used to it.

Chapter Seventeen

ANOTHER WEEK PASSED, AND Caleb continued training at his grandfather's side, fully immersed in the Dark Territory. What he saw still bothered him, but less than it used to.

Torture turned his stomach. Public executions stuck with him longer than he liked. But he was learning how to push the feelings aside.

And each time he did, he felt a little stronger.

No two crimes were handled the same way. Judgment depended entirely on what Ralock and Grandpa decided in the moment. With such a loyal army behind them, their word was law. No one questioned it.

Early one morning, Caleb sat beside his grandfather at the long table in the war room, doing his best to ignore the lingering looks from the head warriors and hunters lining either side. The weekly gathering was underway, filled with updates, orders, and plenty of arguing.

Ralock's seat at the head of the table sat empty once again. Caleb tried not to stare, but he couldn't help but wonder when he would finally meet the man who ruled that land.

A loud caw drew Caleb's attention to the window. A crow was perched on the edge, its black eyes peering in as if it wanted to listen.

Caleb forced himself to look away. The birds patrolled the territory for Ralock, watching for anything that didn't belong.

He resisted the urge to glance back as it cawed again.

Keeping his chin high, Caleb sat still as his grandfather addressed the room. The hateful glares from the military were nothing new. He assumed they were fueled by jealousy. After all, once his training was complete, he would be their leader.

"Why am I still hearing rumors about rebels living in my city?" Grandpa demanded.

The room fell silent. Soldiers exchanged quick glances, but no one spoke.

Grandpa rose slowly from his chair and began pacing the length of the table, his hands clasped behind his back. "Each of you has been trained to track and eliminate traitors like these. So tell me, why are they still here?"

No one answered.

Grandpa turned to Cutler. "You handled the last rebel. What did he tell you?"

"The leader's name is Oliver," Cutler said, the scar along his face tightening as he spoke. "I haven't found him yet."

Grandpa's eyes narrowed. "And why is that?"

"He doesn't bear the mark of the cobra. And he has connections throughout the region."

"Impossible!" Grandpa slammed his fist against the table. "No one lives here without the tattoo."

"He does."

Grandpa's neck reddened as his lips pressed into a thin line. "Find him and bring him to me. I'd like to have a little chat with him."

"Yes, sir." Cutler dipped his head. "I'll find him."

***

Caleb spent most of the day cleaning the barracks and running errands for his grandfather, as he often did. Grandpa gave him a money pouch filled with gold and copper coins, more than enough to cover supplies for both him and the army. Though Caleb still didn't have the cobra tattoo, Grandpa allowed him to wear his cobra ring, which granted him access to any shop in the city.

He didn't have to haul the supplies himself. Instead, he placed orders at the local stores for delivery. Grandpa even allowed him to buy things for himself, something Caleb had never been able to do in his own world.

For the first time in his life, Caleb bought whatever he wanted, and he loved every second of it.

It was late in the afternoon when Caleb finished his tasks and headed back to the barracks, certain his grandfather would be there. As his foot crossed the threshold, the world around him dissolved.

His eyes slammed shut as a vision crashed into him. Suddenly, he was no longer in the barracks but seated inside a modest living room, surrounded by a small group of people listening intently to a woman who spoke with zeal and confidence. Her brown curls bounced as she moved, her voice steady as she spoke of freedom and liberty. Caleb didn't recognize her, but one thing was clear.

She was the rebel leader.

Then, just as suddenly as it had begun, the vision vanished.

His eyes flew open. He was back in the barracks.

Breathing hard, he grabbed the wall to steady himself. His pulse thundered in his ears. The rebel leader was a woman. The realization rattled him. Why had he been shown that?

The image stayed with him as he followed the sound of his grandfather's voice booming down the hallway. His body moved, but his mind kept replaying the scene over and over.

But when he entered the study, he stopped dead in his tracks.

Cutler stood near the center of the room, gripping the arm of a teenage boy who looked to be about seventeen. His face was bruised, and his torn clothes were bloodied.

Recognition hit Caleb like a blow.

He was one of the people from the vision.

He had a similar build to Caleb and appeared to be healthy, with brown hair and matching eyes, but there was something different about him compared to the other followers Caleb had seen. He showed no fear. Even in custody, he stood straight with his chin held high.

"Here's the rebel leader you've been looking for," Cutler said, squaring his shoulders.

"Excellent work, Cutler."

Grandpa looked at the teenager with open interest, his smile slow and calculating. "So," he said, his tone measured, "you're the one who's been causing so many problems in my territory."

The teenager didn't speak. He stared straight ahead.

Caleb knew, without knowing how, that this boy wasn't the leader. And despite himself, compassion tugged at him. He wanted to help.

"He isn't the leader," Caleb said, stepping farther into the room.

Cutler pivoted toward him, his eyes flashing. "How dare you question my authority?"

A slow shiver rolled down Caleb's back, but he kept his voice level. "The person you're looking for is a woman."

"A woman?" Cutler scoffed. "The rebel we captured told me his leader was a man named Oliver."

"He lied to you."

"And how would you know that?" Cutler asked, his eyes hardening.

"I just saw her," Caleb said.

Cutler stepped forward, but Grandpa lifted a hand, stopping him cold.

"Explain yourself, Caleb."

Caleb shifted under their stares. "I...I sometimes have visions."

"Visions?" Grandpa's brows rose.

"I can't control them," Caleb said, looking uncomfortably around the room. "But they show me things. And I just had one...of the rebel leader."

Grandpa studied him carefully. "Who is she?"

"I don't know," Caleb admitted. "She had curly brown hair. She was speaking to five people inside a house. But I know she's the leader. Not him."

"He's lying," Cutler growled.

"I'm not lying," Caleb fired back. "What I see is accurate."

"Silence!"

The single word cut through the room, and every head turned toward Grandpa.

He stood still as he tapped a finger lightly against his chin, weighing his next move. "Caleb," he said, "take the prisoner and lock him in the holding cells. I need to speak with Cutler."

A wave of concern passed through Caleb, but he didn't hesitate. He took hold of the young man's arm and led him from the room. The prisoner's hands were bound behind his back, and Caleb was certain he wouldn't have any trouble transporting him.

The teenager didn't speak as Caleb guided him down the narrow steps into the underground jail. The place was empty. Stale air clung to the bare walls as dim lights flickered overhead.

Caleb shoved him into the first cell and slammed the metal door shut.

"You're not one of them," the teenager said from behind the bars.

"Yes, I am," Caleb shot back.

"No, you're not." He shook his head, his brown hair shifting. "I can see it in your eyes."

"You don't know anything."

"I've been here a lot longer than you," he said, holding Caleb's gaze. "Take my advice and leave while you still can. There's no getting out once he captures you."

"I'm not leaving." Caleb crossed his arms. "My grandfather is one of the leaders. He's training me to become one."

"Don't be fooled," he said. He stepped back and sat down on the stone slab nestled against the wall. "Ralock is the only leader here."

Caleb tilted his head, studying him. Why isn't he afraid? "Cutler is going to kill you."

"I'm not afraid of death," he replied. "That's why I came here."

Caleb didn't look away. "How did you get inside this territory?"

"Snuck in."

"Why?" Caleb pressed. "If you become Ralock's follower and obey his rules, you could live here without trouble."

The young man frowned. "You're so clueless."

"You're the one behind bars," Caleb said through clenched teeth. "Not me."

"The prison you're in is way worse than mine."

Caleb turned and left, anger burning in his chest as he climbed the steps two at a time. He refused to look back.

The next morning, he ate a quick breakfast alone in the penthouse before heading straight to the barracks. He hadn't slept at all. No matter how hard he tried, the prisoner's words kept resurfacing.

Caleb slowed as he descended the dark steps into the cold holding area. He had questions...too many that only the boy could answer. But when he reached the row of cells, his breath caught.

They were empty. The teenager was gone.

Caleb spun and bolted up the stairs. As he rounded the corner, he nearly collided with his grandfather, who was holding a cup of coffee.

"Watch where you're going," he said sharply, grimacing at the fresh stain on his pants.

"Sorry. I didn't see you."

The anger disappeared from his face in an instant, a grin taking its place. "No worries, Little Wilder."

"Where's the prisoner?" Caleb asked. "He isn't in his cell."

"Executed," Grandpa said without hesitation. "Cutler questioned him last night."

"Why?" Caleb's stomach dropped. "He wasn't the leader."

"Doesn't matter; he was a rebel."

Grandpa walked away and disappeared into his study, leaving Caleb alone in the hallway.

Caleb didn't follow. He couldn't.

He's dead.

He rubbed his jaw, replaying every word from the night before. He hadn't liked the teenager, but there had been something about him. His boldness. His calm demeanor. The way he hadn't been afraid. He was unlike anyone Caleb had met in the Dark Territory. Caleb had planned to question him again, to ask why he'd come here in the first place.

Now there would be no answers.

The thought bothered him, but only briefly. There were consequences for breaking the law. The rebel had made his choice.

Chapter Eighteen

Time went on, and with each passing day, Caleb felt stronger. More powerful. The Dark Territory welcomed him, shaped him, taught him how to rule and reign over its people. And he thrived on it.

He lived like a king. Anything he wanted was given to him without question. Jewelry. Clothing. Nothing was off-limits. His grandfather's spare bedroom had become his own, filled with all his luxuries. Grandpa had even promised him a place of his own someday, once he accepted the tattoo, but Caleb saw no reason to rush. He already had everything he desired.

What intrigued him most was how tightly the territory was controlled. No one left without Ralock's permission. Not the warriors. Not the hunters. No exceptions.

Except him.

Caleb could return to his world whenever he wished. No approval was needed. He assumed it was because he was related to Grandpa.

Whatever the reason, it made him feel special.

He rarely returned to his own world. When he did, Jesse, Henry, or Godfrey were already there, waiting—always with the same warnings. He shut those conversations down quickly. Whatever bond they'd once shared no longer mattered.

They had lied to him once already. He wasn't about to listen to them again.

And though Caleb was free to come and go as he pleased, he had seen what happened when others tried to do the same.

Ralock's followers who attempted to leave without permission never made it far. On more than one occasion, Caleb had assisted the hunters in tracking them down, watching as they were dragged back and beaten senseless for their disobedience. Their punishment was swift and brutal. Caleb didn't understand why they hadn't simply asked for approval.

But he never questioned it. He followed orders.

***

Caleb felt the weight of his pocket watch strike against his thigh as he trudged through the bare winter forest, heading toward the Dark Territory. It was December in his world, and the cold here mirrored it perfectly. The air was sharp, biting at his skin, but it was nothing compared to the suffocating life he'd left behind.

That house.

Those rules.

That family.

He welcomed the ache in his legs as he stomped through the frozen leaves. Anything was better than sitting under the Williamses' roof, where he had to bite his tongue and stay out of the way.

He was already in a foul mood, his thoughts circling the argument he'd had with Molly earlier that day. Her voice still rang in his ears—accusatory, demanding, desperate for a version of him that no longer existed. He shoved it aside. She didn't understand him. None of them did.

The irritation faded as anticipation took over.

For weeks, his grandfather had pressed him about the cobra tattoo, and today, Caleb had finally decided to accept it. The thought sent a spark of excitement through him. As a reward, he had been promised that he would finally meet Ralock face-to-face and rule alongside him and Grandpa.

The idea made his pulse quicken.

He was still imagining what the future might look like when he reached the cliff that overlooked the field of poppy flowers.

Godfrey stood at the edge, his red hair lifting in the breeze.

Caleb stopped and crossed his arms. "What do you want, Godfrey?"

"This is your last warning, Caleb," Godfrey said, tucking his hands into his jacket pockets. "If you walk into the Dark Territory today, you won't be able to leave it."

"Yeah, right." Caleb laughed and brushed past him. "My grandfather is a leader there. I can do whatever I want."

"This isn't a game," Godfrey called after him. "Your grandfather was a good man. Nothing like the monster you've been spending time with."

"Great talking to you," Caleb said without slowing. He lifted a mocking hand over his shoulder. "I'll tell Grandpa you said hello."

Godfrey didn't try to stop him as Caleb made his way down the steep trail into the flowers. Before crossing the boundary line, he glanced back. Godfrey was still standing on the cliff, watching him.

Caleb rolled his eyes, then turned away and stepped into the Dark Territory.

***

Caleb pushed his way through the crowd flooding the cobblestone road, shoving people aside as he headed toward his grandfather, who stood atop the large gallows in the center of the city square. The city hummed around him with loud chatter, bartering, and the shuffle of countless feet. It was always crowded at this hour.

"Move!" Caleb barked, shoving a man in the back.

The graying man spun around with a snarl, but Caleb didn't slow. He pushed past him without a second glance, continuing toward the wooden platform used for announcements, public gatherings, and hangings.

Caleb wasn't sure why Grandpa had insisted on meeting him there. A hunter had intercepted him as he entered the Dark Territory and handed him a letter bearing his grandfather's seal. Grandpa's letter offered no explanation beyond a single instruction.

Meet me at the gallows.

Caleb hadn't wasted any time. He dashed through the mountain tunnel and into the busy city, weaving through the people until he reached the square.

For once, there wasn't a body hanging from the gallows as he approached the platform.

Grandpa was already locked in a heated argument with a warrior. That wasn't surprising. It happened often. With a sharp slap across the man's face, Grandpa ordered him to leave, then turned his attention to Caleb like nothing had happened.

"Ah, Caleb, my boy. Perfect timing," he said, offering a hand. "Come on up."

Accepting it with a smirk, Caleb climbed onto the stage and took his place beside his grandfather. "Why did you want to meet me here?"

"The last time you visited, you mentioned wanting the cobra tattoo," Grandpa said, smiling.

"I do." Caleb looked past his grandfather toward the tattoo parlor down the street. "But shouldn't we have met there instead?"

Grandpa chuckled. "That won't be necessary."

"What do you mean?"

"This isn't a typical tattoo." Grandpa wrapped an arm around Caleb's shoulders as he turned them toward the bustling marketplace. He raised his voice until it boomed across the square. "Attention, followers! My grandson has decided to join us."

Most of the irritated townspeople ignored him and went on with their day, but a few slowed, then stopped. Curiosity drew them closer. Soon, a small group gathered around the gallows, waiting to see what would happen.

Caleb glanced around at the twenty-some followers forming a loose circle around them. Jitters stirred in his stomach. Not from fear, but from anticipation. This was it. He was finally getting what he'd longed for: power, respect, and authority.

"Roll up your sleeve," Grandpa said.

Caleb shrugged out of his jacket and tossed it aside before pushing up the sleeve of his long-sleeved shirt. Goosebumps rippled down his arm. He wasn't sure if it was from the cold or his nerves. Whatever the reason, he kept a straight face. He didn't want to look like a coward.

Grandpa reached into the pocket of his fleece jacket and pulled out a small capsule no bigger than a vitamin. Dark liquid swirled inside it. "Swallow this."

Caleb cocked an eyebrow as he plucked the pill from his grandfather's wrinkled palm. "I thought I was getting a tattoo."

"You are. Once you take it, the cobra will form on your forearm."

Caleb held the pill up with two fingers, watching the black liquid move. Godfrey's warning came to mind, lingering longer than it should have.

What if Godfrey was telling the truth?

The crowd began to cheer. Fists pumped the air as boots thundered against the cobblestones, and the roar smothered his worry. He tossed the capsule into his mouth and forced it down his dry throat.

At first, nothing happened. Then pain exploded inside him like he'd swallowed a bomb. Heat tore down his arm as his veins bulged and turned black.

Caleb screamed as the cobra tattoo began to carve itself into his forearm, dark lines burning through his skin while the crowd erupted in applause. He clenched his jaw, tears blurring his vision, as he endured the worst pain he had ever known. Finally, the pain eased, leaving the cobra perfectly etched into his arm.

His grandfather seized his wrist and lifted the tattooed arm high into the air.

The horde of followers went wild, shouting and crashing into one another like a pack of rowdy football players before a big game. Though pain still pulsed through him, Caleb felt something else rising beneath it.

Power.

He raised his other arm in triumph.

While the crowd was still hooting and hollering, Grandpa leaned in close and whispered in Caleb's ear, "You're mine now."

His fingers dug deeper into Caleb's wrist until the pain became unbearable.

"That hurts, Grandpa."

Grandpa released him with a dark, bellowing laugh and turned back to the crowd. "He still thinks I'm his grandfather."

The crowd laughed as Grandpa's body began to convulse.

Caleb stumbled back, horror rooting him in place as the man before him twisted and changed until his grandfather was gone. In his place stood a young, lean man with short black hair. His face was clean-shaven, his features sharp and handsome, and he wore a black suit threaded with faint gold streaks that seemed to move as if the fabric were alive.

"Who are you?" Caleb breathed, stumbling backward.

"I'm Ralock," the man said. His pitch-black eyes bore into Caleb. "Your new master."

Caleb went pale. "Where's my grandfather?"

Ralock released another horrific laugh. "He wants to know where his grandfather is," he mocked, scanning the bustling crowd as they burst into laughter. "Your grandfather is dead."

"You tricked me!"

"You will not speak to me in that tone," Ralock growled.

Without warning, he backhanded Caleb across the face. The blow sent him tumbling off the platform and into the crowd below. No one moved to catch him. He slammed into the cobblestones.

Pain seared across his cheek as he pushed himself upright. When he looked up, Ralock was staring down at him, amused.

"Let that be a lesson to all of you," Ralock said to the crowd. "Disrespect will not be tolerated."

The crowd quickly dispersed, the square emptying until Caleb was left alone on the ground.

Ralock jumped down from the platform and crouched beside him. "There's no sense in trying to escape, boy," he said, a mocking smile tugging at his lips. "You'll never make it out alive."

Ralock's dark laughter echoed in Caleb's ears as he walked away, leaving him behind.

No one helped. No one even looked at him.

Caleb dragged himself up, staring at the snake blistering across his forearm. Dizzy and unfocused, he stumbled into the busy street. His thoughts were foggy, and his body ached like he'd been drugged. He veered sideways, fighting to keep his balance as his head throbbed.

Somehow, he managed to stagger through the mountain tunnel and into the woods. He followed the trail that led toward the poppy field, each step heavier than the last.

Roots and dead brush snagged at his boots as he pressed toward the border, his legs barely steady beneath him. Every movement sent pain flaring through his arm, but he kept going.

Godfrey's warning resurfaced. *You won't be able to leave.*

He gritted his teeth and kept moving.

Red flowers appeared ahead, threading between the bare winter trees. The poppies bent and swayed in the cold air as he pressed forward.

He fixed his gaze on them and didn't slow despite the growing pain.

"Where do you think you're going?" a rough voice asked from behind him.

Terror gripped Caleb as he turned and saw a hunter descending from a watchtower.

He was in the red zone. A place no follower was allowed to enter.

Caleb had been here before. He had even helped the hunters patrol it, but now he understood the truth. It had all been a lie, and he was in real danger.

"Nice tattoo," the hunter said, stepping closer. "Looks like our master finally claimed you."

Caleb stared at the hunter's camouflaged face, his body trembling. He knew what they were capable of. He had to get away.

His thoughts swarmed, but one fact cut through the fog: the hunters couldn't leave the territory without Ralock's permission.

If he could reach the border—

He didn't finish the thought.

Caleb broke into a desperate run toward the tree line. Pain shot through his arm as his boots pounded against the frozen ground. His breath turned ragged as he shouted the only name he could think of.

"Godfrey!"

He didn't make it far.

The hunter tackled him from behind, slamming Caleb into the dirt and knocking the wind from his lungs. Though Caleb was strong and knew how to fight, his body felt sluggish and useless as the hunter's fist crashed into his face.

Stars burst across his vision as he collapsed, unable to move.

The hunter laughed, grabbing a fistful of Caleb's hair and dragging him deeper into the territory. Caleb kicked and swung blindly, but his limbs failed him as his body scraped across the forest floor.

"Jesse!" he screamed. "Help me!"

Caleb kept shouting, but his pleas only fueled the hunter's laughter as he was dragged farther from freedom. By the time his voice gave out, the truth finally dawned on him.

He had made a terrible mistake.

Chapter Nineteen

THE PIERCING SHRIEKS OF hungry crows jolted Caleb awake the next day. He slowly pried open his heavy eyes, only to be blinded by the sun hanging high overhead.

He rubbed his throbbing head; his skull pounded as if it might split apart. What had happened? Everything was hazy.

Leaning back against a cold brick wall, he took in his surroundings. The quiet street was unfamiliar, but the rows of old brick homes told him enough. He was in the city.

How did I get here?

As Caleb scanned the empty street, his forearm suddenly ignited like it had been doused in gasoline and set aflame. A low groan escaped him as he looked down.

He froze.

The cobra tattoo.

The memories hit him all at once: the choice he'd made, the searing pain, Ralock.

Horror clamped down on him as he staggered to his feet, fear tearing through him. He clutched the iron bars guarding the window to keep himself upright. The cold metal stung his palms as he caught sight of his reflection.

He cringed. He looked as awful as he felt.

Dried vomit clung to the corner of his mouth, and dark circles sagged beneath his bloodshot eyes. An ugly bruise bloomed across his cheek, and his skin was cracked and raw from the bitter cold.

What have I done?

Panic set in.

He had no coins. No way to buy food, water, or supplies. He needed shelter, a place to sleep, and protection from followers who would kill for a scrap of bread. With nothing but the clothes on his back, he wouldn't last long in the Dark Territory.

Caleb's head jerked up at the sound of footsteps. A young man was heading straight toward him.

"Please," Caleb said, desperation cracking his voice. "Help me."

The man walked right past him without even a glance, his dark trench coat flapping behind him.

Caleb swallowed back the lump in his throat. He was one of them now—the people he'd ignored and avoided, the ones he'd never helped while he spent his coins on himself.

"I'm such an idiot." He dragged a hand over his face and sank down onto the filthy sidewalk.

A broken sob tore from his chest as he buried his face in his hands, the weight of his choice suffocating him.

He'd been lied to. Manipulated.

He wasn't special. He was just another follower under Ralock's control.

Escaping suddenly felt impossible.

***

Caleb stared ahead, his face drained of emotion.

Adeline couldn't take her eyes off him. Her heart ached as the pieces settled into place. Ralock hadn't just deceived him. He'd broken him.

"I don't know how long I was there," Caleb said. "I stopped keeping track after the first year." He fell silent, rubbing his swollen knuckles. "It felt like forever."

He exhaled slowly through his nose. "I tried to escape, but they always found me," he continued, his words eerily steady. "I'm lucky they didn't kill me."

Silence stretched between them.

Adeline let the quiet linger. She could see the toll etched across his face. Remembering forced him to relive things he'd never truly escaped. Telling his story was costing him far more than she'd first assumed.

Caleb finally looked at her, something dark flaring in his good eye. "If Godfrey, Henry, and Jesse are so great, why didn't they come for me?" His hand curled into a fist. "I begged for help, but they never came."

Adeline braced herself, searching for the right words. "They did warn you," she said, tucking her damp hair behind her ears. "But you didn't believe them."

"I know I should've listened!" he snapped. "But you'd think they would've forgiven me. Saved me. Knowing what I went through."

Adeline bit her bottom lip, her mind scrambling for a response. One wrong word could set him off.

"I think they wanted to," she said softly. "But they had to honor your choice. You went into the Dark Territory. You accepted Ralock's mark."

Caleb stiffened. He opened his mouth as if to argue, then closed it when no words came. He looked away.

"Jesse died to save you, Caleb." She wiped her tear-filled eyes. "If it weren't for him, you'd still be chained up in that basement."

"I didn't ask him to save me that time."

"You didn't have to." Her voice broke. "Jesse cared about you, just like I know Godfrey and Henry do. From the moment we saw you with those wolves, he couldn't stop talking about how important you were."

Caleb glanced at her, surprised. "He did?"

"Yes." A small, strained smile touched her lips. "I disagreed with him...a lot. But he didn't care. He told me to give you a chance."

"That sounds like the Jesse I used to know." Caleb let out a shaky laugh as moisture gathered in his eye.

"And you know what?" Tears slipped down her cheeks. "He was right."

The words shattered something inside Caleb. A sob ripped from his throat as he covered his bruised face with shaking hands. His shoulders folded inward as he rocked back and forth, the raw sound of grief filling the room.

Adeline remained still, fighting the swell of emotion. She squeezed her eyes shut as tears spilled freely down her face. Jesse's death hung between them, an unspoken weight neither of them could escape.

Caleb's cries slowly softened, but the grief didn't lift. It lingered in the small space between them, binding them together in a way words never could.

Adeline couldn't imagine a life without Jesse.

But one thing was certain: Caleb had loved him just as much as she had.

Chapter Twenty

Eventually, Adeline and Caleb moved into the kitchen. They ate a quiet lunch together, simple sandwiches that were left mostly untouched. Adeline made herself eat despite the knot in her stomach.

They didn't speak much.

Adeline's thoughts kept circling back to everything Caleb had already shared, and everything he hadn't. She'd heard enough about the Dark Territory to know it was worse than anything she'd imagined, and the thought of him living there for so long made her chest ache.

Whatever came next, she knew it wouldn't be easy to hear. But she had to know.

"What did you do after you woke up in the city?" Adeline asked, turning on the barstool to face him.

"I don't remember much." Caleb kept his head down, staring at his plate. "Not those first few days." His fingers curled against the edge of the plate. "I just remember being cold. And hungry."

He drifted into silence for a long while, his attention no longer in the room. His shoulders tensed as the present slipped away.

***

Caleb shoved a branch aside as he pushed through the forest, his lungs burning as he stumbled over roots and low brush. His boots crashed into the hard earth as the pit of his stomach tightened with every step. He was close to the border.

Fear clawed at him, demanding that he turn back. To run the other way. But he refused to listen.

He was tired of being cold. Tired of eating scraps from trash cans. He had to leave.

Without warning, Ralock appeared out of thin air a few yards in front of Caleb. He wore a black three-piece suit threaded with streaks of gold and had a sword strapped to his back.

Crossing his arms, he smirked. "Going somewhere?"

Caleb jerked to a halt, his breath catching as his knees knocked together. Two hunters stepped out from the trees behind Ralock, their yellow eyes bright against their camouflaged faces. Terror coursed through him.

"I thought I made myself clear," Ralock said, his voice smooth and mocking. "You're my property now. You don't get to leave."

Caleb took a step back, his mind reeling. *How did they find me?*

He'd chosen this place because it was secluded. It was away from patrols and watchtowers. He knew they had advanced technology. He'd seen it. But how were they tracking him?

It didn't matter now. They'd found him.

He pivoted and bolted in the opposite direction.

"Get him!" Ralock roared.

The hunters tore after Caleb, leaving Ralock behind. Caleb crashed through the trees, leaping fallen logs and dodging branches that clawed at him.

He was fast, had always been fast, but speed couldn't save him.

Hands caught him from behind, and he hit the ground hard.

They wrestled on the ground, but once the second hunter joined the fight, it was over. A fist slammed into Caleb's face, snapping his head to the side before he was hauled to his feet.

The world spun as one of the hunters clamped down on his arm, hard enough to bruise.

"You're a very stupid boy." Ralock approached, unhurried. "You know that you can't outsmart me or my military."

Caleb stayed silent, pain pulsing through his face.

Ralock seized his chin, his claws biting into his flesh as he forced him to look up. "There's no sense in running." He leaned in, his lips grazing Caleb's ear. "I will find you. Every time."

Ralock released his chin and struck. His knuckles slammed into Caleb's gut, knocking the air from his lungs.

Caleb doubled over, gasping, but the hunters yanked him upright before he could collapse.

"Have at him, boys," Ralock said, already turning away.

The hunters wasted no time. Fists and boots hammered into Caleb without restraint. Pain came in relentless waves until it was impossible to tell where one blow ended and the next began.

They left him crumpled on the cold forest floor.

Caleb lay face down in the dirt, blood pooling in his mouth as agony detonated through him. He pressed his palms to the earth and tried to pull himself up, but his body trembled and collapsed beneath him.

"Help me, Henry," he whispered.

Then everything went dark.

***

Hours after the sun had set, Caleb awoke to a soft touch shaking his shoulder. He groaned, his body protesting as he sluggishly pried his swollen eyes open.

A woman knelt beside him. The darkness swallowed her features, leaving only a vague silhouette hovering in his blurred vision. Panic jolted through him. Was she one of Ralock's followers there to finish him off?

"My name is Olivia," the woman whispered, tossing a quick glance over her shoulder. "I'm here to help you."

Caleb couldn't keep his eyes open. His mind struggled to grasp who Olivia was. He didn't know anyone by that name.

"Can you walk?" she asked.

"I don't know. Everything hurts."

"You must try," she said, tugging him upward. "I won't be able to carry you to my cottage."

It took Caleb a few seconds before he could stand. Even then, his body swayed, threatening to give out as the cold seeped into his bones. Pain flared all over as Olivia slipped his arm over her shoulders and steadied him before he could fall. She was much shorter than him, but clearly strong.

Who was this woman?

Despite Olivia's best efforts, helping Caleb walk was a struggle. He groaned with every step as they stumbled through the dark forest. The uneven ground was nearly impossible to navigate in his condition.

The throbbing in his ribs and face consumed his thoughts as he let the woman who saved him lead him into the unknown. He wasn't sure where they were going, but he no longer cared.

With no sense of how long they'd been walking, Caleb drifted in and out of consciousness until he finally stumbled out of the woods with Olivia. She guided him past a row of small brick homes dimly lit by the moonlight.

Caleb recognized the area at once as they approached the last cottage, surrounded by trees. He'd passed this part of the city many times. It was near one of the barracks, but he'd never stepped inside any of the homes fortified with iron bars across their windows and doors.

They moved through the backyard and down a short brick walkway. Olivia unlocked the iron bars protecting the back door, then opened it and helped Caleb inside. She steered him through the dark room until they reached a couch. He winced as he sank down onto it.

"Rest," Olivia said, placing a blanket over him. "You're safe for now."

Caleb had no idea who she was, and in that moment, he didn't care. The sudden warmth and exhaustion pulled him under the second his eyes closed.

Chapter Twenty-One

A vicious headache ripped Caleb from his nightmare. He bolted upright, sweat slicking his skin as he scanned the room for the demon that had been chasing him.

It wasn't there.

He was alone in a small living area, everything neat and in its place. The room smelled faintly of old wood and ash. It wasn't impressive, but it carried a simple comfort that reminded him of his old home with Grandpa.

Caleb rubbed his pounding head. He felt like he'd been hit by a bus.

"You're lucky it's only bruises and cuts." Olivia stepped into the living room from the hallway. "It could've been a lot worse."

Caleb turned toward her, his neck aching. Brown curls brushed her shoulders as she moved with a tight and serious expression. She looked to be in her late thirties, small and petite, but there was nothing fragile about her. A toughness clung to her, the kind that made Caleb uneasy.

And the longer he stared, the more certain he became that he'd seen her before. But where?

One thing was certain: she intimidated him. There was a discipline to her movements and a confidence that suggested she'd seen real combat. She wasn't someone he wanted to cross.

As Olivia moved past him and into the adjoining kitchen, Caleb caught a glimpse of a sharp knife resting at her hip. It was partially hidden beneath a black leather jacket that would do little against the cold.

Caleb tensed. Where had she gotten that? Outside weapons weren't permitted in the Dark Territory, only the solid black blades carried by Ralock and his military.

And she certainly wasn't one of them.

The realization only fueled Caleb's curiosity. How had she managed to hide the knife from the hunters and warriors who would have confiscated it without hesitation?

Whatever the answer was, it would have to wait.

Olivia returned with a cup of water and handed it to him. "Here."

Caleb accepted it as she eased into the recliner across from him.

"What's your name?" she asked, watching him closely.

"Caleb." He took a sip of water.

Olivia remained still, studying him with an intensity that made his skin prickle.

Caleb lowered his eyes, avoiding her gaze.

"You can stay here as long as you like," she finally said, leaning back and crossing her arms. "I have an extra bedroom."

Caleb's head shot up, his brows drawing together. Generosity didn't exist in Ralock's land. What did she want from him?

He searched her stern face, trying to decide whether this was another trap. Again, he couldn't tell. But she had saved him, and that had to count for something.

"I don't have anything to give you besides a pocket watch," he said, reaching into his pocket to show her.

"I don't want anything from you."

A tide of emotion rose too fast to stop. Blinking back sudden tears, Caleb dropped his eyes to the floor. No one had been kind to him since he'd received Ralock's mark. "Why are you helping me?"

"Because I can." Olivia stood. "I'll put some clean sheets on your bed. Feel free to take a shower; it's the second door on your left."

She gestured toward the hallway to the left of the fireplace before heading back into the kitchen.

Caleb lifted the glass and finished the water, then set it on the end table beside him.

The thought of a long, hot shower was enough to make him push himself up from the worn couch. He hadn't bathed in days, and he smelled just as bad as the garbage bins he'd been scavenging from.

He struggled down the narrow hallway and into a small bathroom that smelled of mildew. The outdated light fixture above the mirror hummed softly as he looked up.

Caleb recoiled. He barely recognized the man staring back at him. His right eye was swollen, dark, and bruised beyond recognition. Deep purple and black bruises marred his face, along with several gashes from the punches he'd taken the night before.

At least they didn't knock out my teeth.

His grandfather had paid a small fortune for braces when Caleb was in middle school. It would be a shame for that investment to go to waste.

Not that it mattered anymore. In the Dark Territory, even basic hygiene was a luxury. A toothbrush and toothpaste cost more coins than he had to his name.

He pushed the thought away. That was a problem for another day.

Caleb groaned as he peeled off his tattered shirt and tossed it in the corner. He was still in decent shape, though leaner than before. He frowned. That would change.

He winced as he examined the bruises covering most of his body. Some were small, others the size of a fist. The pain was nearly unbearable, but at least the hunters hadn't used their knives like they usually did.

The thought sent a shiver through him as he grabbed a towel from beneath the sink and hung it on the hook near the shower. It was rough and old, riddled with a few holes, but it was clean. He pushed the shower curtain aside and turned on the water.

He finished undressing and stepped into the shower, sighing as warm water cascaded over him. It sank into his aching bones as he lathered on the body wash, its earthy scent filling the small space.

The grime washed away easily, but the hopelessness did not. It clung to him, whispering that he was trapped in the Dark Territory for good.

His thoughts drifted to his girlfriend, Molly, and the last conversation they'd shared. The fight. The words he wished he could take back. He ran a hand through his short blond hair, wondering if he would ever see her again.

Knock. Knock. Knock.

The abrupt sound snapped him out of his thoughts and sent his heart racing. He peeked out from behind the shower curtain and watched the closed door. "Yeah?"

"I have some clean clothes that will probably fit you," Olivia said, her words muffled. "I'll leave them outside the door."

Why does she have clothes that fit me?

"Okay," he called back, the steam curling around him

Caleb felt a little better as he dried off and changed into the clothes Olivia had left for him. The sweats fit perfectly.

He entered the living area and found Olivia in the recliner, a book open in her hands. Sunlight rested on her as she read. There was a peacefulness about her that felt strange, almost wrong.

In this territory, everyone was either hostile or depressed. She was neither.

Olivia lowered her novel. A strange look crossed her face. "I'm glad they fit."

"Me too," he said, sitting across from her. "Thanks."

"You're welcome." She gave a slight nod. "How are you feeling?"

"Pretty rough."

"Time will help."

He drew a slow breath. "I doubt it. Ralock made it pretty clear I can't leave."

"Escaping won't be easy, but it *is* possible. I know people who've done it."

"How?" he asked, desperation clear in his voice. "Every time I get close to the territory line, Ralock and his hunters find me."

"That's because your blood is tainted with a tracking device."

He paled. "What?"

"The black pill you swallowed didn't just create the cobra tattoo. It polluted your blood, so Ralock can always track you. That's why the hunters are so precise when someone tries to escape."

Caleb shook his head as dread took over. "I had no idea."

"That's the point," she said. "Only Ralock and his army know."

"Then how do *you* know?"

Olivia's mouth curved into a faint, knowing smile. "Let's just say I have connections. I know things most people don't."

"So how does anyone escape?"

"Most people don't. If you truly want out, you'll have to fight for it. No matter how many times you fail." She paused. "The hardest part will be breaking past the territory line. Once you do, you can't slow down. You'll have to put as much distance between yourself and this place as possible. Ralock will send hunters after you, but the farther you get, the harder it will be for them to catch you—especially if you're armed and know how to defend yourself."

The truth crashed down on him. How would he ever escape?

"Why doesn't Ralock just kill escapees?" Caleb asked. "Wouldn't that be easier than dragging them back?"

"He sometimes does," she said. "But he gains power from anyone who willingly takes the tattoo. If he kills them, he loses that power."

"How?"

"I don't know." She shrugged. "But I do know he tricks and threatens people into getting it."

"Is there any way to get rid of the tattoo?"

"Not that I know of."

Caleb ran a hand over his face. "So, you're basically saying I'm screwed."

"I never said that." Olivia's gaze was unflinching. "I want you to understand what you're risking if you try to escape again. The beating you took yesterday was nothing compared to what I've seen."

Caleb leaned back against the couch and exhaled sharply as guilt hit him like a blow. He knew exactly what she was talking about. He hadn't just witnessed horrific punishments; he'd been a part of them.

"You don't act like one of Ralock's followers," he said, eager to shift his thoughts elsewhere.

"Because I'm not one."

"What?"

"I blend in." She folded her hands in her lap. "When I'm out, I act like everyone else. Stern. Harsh. Dangerous if I need to be. That's the only way to survive here."

"How do you buy supplies without the tattoo?"

She smirked. "I have connections all over the city. People willing to barter. I can get whatever I need."

"But how do you stay under Ralock's radar? He has entire teams that hunt down and kill outsiders. Even the crows help him."

"Because they expect outsiders to stand out, especially in the city. I make sure I don't."

Caleb studied her face, a strange familiarity settling over him. He'd seen her before...somewhere.

Something tugged at the back of his mind. Then it clicked.

"Wait. I know you." His eyes widened. "You're the rebel leader Ralock's been searching for."

Olivia dipped her chin. "I am."

"They think your name is Oliver."

"That's my alias. It makes them assume I'm a man."

"That's clever." A half-smile tugged at his mouth. "But why would you want to stay here if you don't have to?"

"I have my reasons, Caleb."

Caleb waited for her to elaborate, but she didn't. He couldn't fathom why anyone would choose to live there.

As his thoughts drifted, a memory surfaced. The teenage boy. The rebel Cutler had captured and executed.

"Who was the teenager they caught?" Caleb asked.

For a while, Olivia said nothing as she looked away.

"Hector," she finally whispered. "He was my son."

The room went silent as Caleb reeled back, realization hitting him. He could see the resemblance now. "He was brave," he said at last.

"I know." She wiped her eyes. "But sometimes bravery gets you killed."

Caleb stared at the floor, a lump rising in his throat.

"Living here isn't going to be easy for you," she said, straightening. "But no matter what happens, you cannot lose hope."

"Hope?" Caleb let out a hollow laugh. "I already lost that."

"Then you won't last long."

Chapter Twenty-Two

The first month in the Dark Territory slipped by as Caleb slowly healed and regained his strength while living with Olivia. He rarely left her cottage. When he did, he made sure she was with him. It was far too dangerous for him to wander alone, especially without a weapon.

"You need to get a job," Olivia said, looking across the table at Caleb as she took a quick swig from her beer.

Caleb nearly choked on his peanut butter sandwich. "You're kidding."

"I'm dead serious." She fixed him with a steady look. "We need the extra coins."

Fear crept up his spine as he shifted in his seat. "How do you even get a job here?"

"There's an employment agency," she said. "They assign work based on your skills."

"Skills?" Caleb huffed. "The only thing I'm good at is sports, and I highly doubt they're hiring for that."

Olivia waved a hand dismissively. "I'm sure you have other useful skills."

Caleb thought for a moment, his mind drifting to his favorite hobby.

"I used to cook a lot," he said, a hint of sadness creeping in as his thoughts turned to Henry Snow. "But I haven't done it in a while."

"Then you're already better than half the chefs here," Olivia said, finishing her beer and setting the bottle down. "Most of them have never cooked a day in their lives."

Caleb didn't reply.

"Come on." Olivia pushed her chair back. "We'd better get going before the city gets too crowded."

Caleb downed the rest of his bland sandwich before hurrying out the door with Olivia. The cold air cut through his jacket, and he pulled it tighter around himself as he struggled to keep up. His stomach churned as they passed the gallows. A new body swayed there. Caleb looked away quickly, forcing his gaze to the miserable faces lining the street instead.

They stopped at a tall, narrow building wedged between a bookstore and a butchery. Olivia paused at the entrance. "I can't go inside with you."

A chill ran through Caleb as the street noise faded. "Why not?"

"I can't risk them asking to see the cobra tattoo," she said, tucking her hands into her leather jacket.

"I don't want to go in alone."

"You have to." Her voice was firm. "I'll wait right here for you."

Caleb swallowed, his hands starting to shake. "What do I say when I'm in there?"

"Just tell them you need a job."

Swearing under his breath, he forced himself to open the glass door and step inside alone.

His palms began to sweat as he glanced over his shoulder to make sure Olivia was still waiting outside before moving toward the front desk.

He was relieved to find the lobby empty. Behind the cluttered desk sat a very old man with deep wrinkles carved into his face. He was painfully skinny with thinning white hair and a hunched frame. The man looked well over a hundred.

Caleb stopped in front of him, every muscle in his body tensing.

The man's eyes lifted behind thin wire-rimmed glasses. "What can I do for you?"

"I need a job."

The man said nothing. He reached into the drawer, retrieved a sheet of paper, and began filling it out without looking up. "Name?"

"Caleb Wilder."

"Age?"

"Eighteen."

"Skills?"

"I can cook," Caleb said, a nervous edge to his voice.

The old man adjusted his glasses and took his time jotting down the information before looking up. "Show me the mark."

Rolling up his sleeve, Caleb revealed the black cobra tattoo, still fresh on his forearm. It no longer burned, but he hated the sight of it. He looked away as the old man gave it a brief glance.

Once the man saw it was legitimate, he stood from his chair and hobbled toward the cabinet behind him. After searching for a bit, he located a massive black book and struggled to pull it free.

Caleb tensed as the man hauled the thick book back to the desk. It looked heavy, and Caleb half expected him to collapse under its weight. Somehow, he managed to settle back into his chair and crack the book open. He flipped through the pages, then paused. "You're lucky, boy."

"Why?"

"Because we've not had any available jobs in your skill set for weeks," he said, glancing up from the book. "But we just received notice that there's an opening at Drop Dead Diner."

Caleb's stomach knotted, but he was careful to keep his face blank. He remembered that place all too well. He could still taste the stale bagel and smell the greasy air that clung to everything. "What's the position?"

"Cook."

"I'll take it. How much does it pay?"

The man squinted at the fine print. "One copper coin every eight-hour shift."

"That's it?"

The man removed his spectacles and set them neatly on the desk. "If you're going to be ungrateful, I'll give it to someone else."

"No, please," Caleb said, the words rushing out before he could stop them. "I'm new here and still learning how things work."

The old man gave him a long, hard stare before picking up his pen. "Fine. The job is yours."

Caleb's heart pounded as he watched the white-haired man fill out a basic application form. When he finished signing it, the man slid the paper across the desk.

"Take this to the diner," he said. "They'll give you further instructions."

The elderly man went back to work as Caleb grabbed the paper and hustled out of the building. A chilly breeze slammed into him, and he spotted Olivia leaning against the brick wall. Her arms were crossed, her expression hard as she scanned the growing crowd before finally looking at him.

"Did you get one?" she asked.

"Yeah." Caleb shivered. "I'll be cooking at Drop Dead Diner."

Olivia's messy curls shifted in the wind as her eyes slid back to the street. Her jaw tightened. She didn't say anything, but the silence told him enough. "When do you start?"

"I'm not sure," Caleb said, lifting the paper. "I have to give them this."

"All right, then." Olivia pushed off the wall. "Let's go."

***

Heat rolled off the stovetop as Caleb flipped a line of burgers as fast as his hands would move. Sweat slicked his skin and his shirt clung to his back as he hustled from the grill to the counter and back again. He'd been on his feet for hours. Every muscle ached, but stopping wasn't an option. If he slowed down, he wouldn't get paid.

"I need that order of fries now!" a waitress shouted through the service window.

"They ain't ready yet, Brenda," the head chef barked. "So shut up!"

"Don't make me come back there!"

Caleb rolled his eyes as his coworkers continued to argue. It wasn't going to stop.

He moved to the fryer, yanked the basket from the oil, and dumped the fries onto a plate. Steam burned his face as he shoved them onto the service hatch, cutting straight through Brenda's rant. "Here."

"Finally." Brenda snatched the plate and stormed off.

The head chef's glare lingered on Caleb, but he ignored it and turned back to the grill. He wasn't about to pick a fight, not when his shift was nearly over.

By the time his shift ended, his muscles throbbed and his patience was gone. He cleaned his station, ditched his apron, and slipped out the back door into the alley.

The night was dreary and cold. Caleb hugged his arms to his chest as he searched for Olivia. She was already there, like always, dressed in black with a cigarette glowing between her fingers. She walked him to and from work every day and night. It wasn't safe for him to walk alone.

The butt of her cigarette glowed as she took a final drag before dropping it to the ground and crushing it beneath her boot. "How was work?"

Caleb didn't answer. He just exhaled slowly, his shoulders sagging as they started down the street. He'd only worked there a couple of weeks and already wanted to quit. The hours were long, the customers were cruel, and every night he left smelling like grease and sweat.

"That bad, huh?" Olivia said.

A foul stench hit them without warning. A sickly girl lunged out from behind a dumpster, a jagged piece of metal clutched in her hand. Her eyes were sunken, her movements twitchy and desperate. "Give me your coins," she hissed through rotted teeth.

Olivia stepped in front of Caleb. "Get out of our way."

"Not until you give me the coins." The girl waved the rusted metal wildly.

Olivia moved with startling speed. She kicked the weapon from the girl's hand, then drove her fist into her mouth. The impact sent her slamming back against the brick wall.

Olivia's knife was out an instant later, the blade pressed tight to the girl's throat. "I'll give you one last chance," she said calmly. "Leave us."

A moment later, Olivia lowered her knife and stepped back. The girl's eyes were wide with fear, blood dripping from her split lip as she scrambled down the dark alley and vanished into the night.

"That was close," Caleb said, finally exhaling.

Olivia tucked her knife out of sight. "She didn't stand a chance. It's the hunters and warriors you need to worry about. Not desperate girls with scrap metal."

"Right," Caleb said as they started walking again. "So when are you going to get me a knife?"

"I'm not."

"Why not?"

"Because if you're caught with it, you'll be questioned and punished," Olivia said, her breath fogging the air. "I won't allow that."

"The same can happen to you."

"I know." Olivia didn't slow her pace. "You don't need to worry about me, Caleb."

Their boots echoed against the cobblestones as they passed beneath a flickering streetlight.

Olivia could take care of herself. Caleb didn't doubt that. But what if Ralock found her?

The thought turned his blood to ice. He couldn't lose her too.

Caleb shoved the fear down as they walked on, hoping it would never come to that.

Chapter Twenty-Three

"I lived with Olivia for a long time," Caleb said, his gaze fixed ahead. "She became like a mother to me."

Adeline stayed silent, letting him take his time.

"She kept me safe. Taught me how to survive. How to stay out of trouble. I wouldn't have lasted long without her."

A heavy ache settled in her chest. The photograph she'd found at the cottage surfaced in her mind. The woman's guarded smile. The teenage boy standing close at her side. It all made sense now. "She sounds like an incredible woman."

"She was."

Silence returned to the kitchen, stretching between them.

Adeline chose her words carefully. "What happened to her?"

Caleb shifted on the barstool. "She disappeared."

***

Rain hammered against the cottage roof, drowning out every other sound. Caleb sat alone in the dim room, his arms wrapped around himself as he watched the storm rage beyond the window.

Olivia should have been home by now. She'd left early that morning to pick up supplies, like she always did. Hours had passed since then, and the sky had only grown darker. Olivia never stayed out this late.

His foot tapped against the floor, faster with each passing second. He glanced at the door, then back at the window. He didn't know what to do. Going outside wasn't safe. Not without a weapon, and Olivia still refused to give him one.

Even with a weapon, Caleb doubted he'd ever go anywhere alone. He only went out with Olivia.

Thunder cracked overhead, making Caleb jump. He tried to steady his breathing as his heart kicked hard against his ribs. Olivia was fine. She had to be. She could handle anything.

Another roll of thunder launched him to his feet. He began to pace.

Olivia always came home before dark. It was well past dusk now.

Caleb crossed the room again and again, weighing his options. He could go out into the storm and search for her...or stay and wait.

Lightning split the sky as rain poured down in sheets. He wouldn't stand a chance out there.

Caleb dragged a hand over his dreadlocks and sank back down onto the couch.

He had to wait.

***

Caleb roused from the couch early the next morning with a dull ache between his eyes. His head felt heavy, as if he hadn't slept at all.

Olivia.

He shoved the blanket aside and hurried down the hallway toward her bedroom. "Olivia!" he called. "Are you here?"

No response.

His heartbeat quickened as he pushed open her bedroom door. He froze, his stomach dropping.

Her bed was empty.

Caleb ran back into the hallway, his voice echoing through the house. "Olivia!"

He checked every room. Opened every door.

She wasn't there.

The truth struck him, stealing the strength from his legs. She had never come home.

Caleb grabbed the wall for support, his breath coming fast and shallow as panic closed in.

Pull yourself together.

He closed his eyes and took a few slow breaths. Little by little, the panic loosened its grip. Fear still twisted his gut as he forced his legs to move. He'd never gone out alone, not without her, but there was no other choice.

He grabbed his winter jacket and pulled the hood over his head. His hands shook as he laced up his boots, nausea rolling through him with every tug.

Whatever was out there, he would face it.

One thought anchored him as he stepped toward the door.

He was going to find Olivia.

Chapter Twenty-Four

Gray clouds hung low over the city, releasing a fine mist over the empty streets. Caleb kept his head down as he moved along the cobblestone walkway, his hands shoved deep into his jacket pockets.

The street was quiet. A little too quiet, but he couldn't let that distract him. His eyes flicked to every doorway, every shadowed corner, searching for any sign of Olivia.

He splashed through the shallow puddles as he turned down another alley. Overloaded trash bins lined the walls, rainwater pooling beneath them. Nothing else.

His breath fogged in the cold air as he kept going. He'd been walking for over an hour now, wandering the streets with no direction and no luck. He'd known it wouldn't be easy. The city was vast, and the woods beyond it stretched even farther.

Caleb tried to convince himself she was fine, but with each passing minute, it became harder to believe. What if she had been captured? What if he was already too late?

He shoved the questions away and kept moving. The cold burned his nose and cheeks, and his stomach rumbled in protest, but he didn't slow down. Quitting wasn't an option.

As he approached the next alleyway, his heart leaped. A woman sat slumped against a brick wall, her head bowed. She was about Olivia's size, but her brown hair hung in wet strands over her face, hiding her features.

Caleb sprinted down the alley and dropped to his knees in front of her. She didn't react. He reached out and gently shook her shoulder. "Olivia?"

The woman slowly lifted her head, wet strands of hair falling away from her face. Caleb recoiled. Open sores blotted her skin, stretching across a broad nose and a face deeply lined with age.

The woman's lips pulled into a toothless grin. A harsh, rattling laugh spilled from her throat. "You should've stayed away."

Caleb scrambled backward and lost his footing. He landed hard on the ground, icy water seeping into his pants.

Before he could get away, she lunged. Something sharp flashed in her hand as she slammed her weight onto him. Freezing water soaked through his jacket as he struggled beneath her. He tried to shove her off, but she was stronger than she looked.

A burst of pain tore through his stomach.

Caleb gasped as she ripped the jagged shard of glass free, blood spilling across his side. He clamped his hand over the wound. The pressure sent a violent surge of agony through him as he lay there, helpless, listening to her laugh.

Warm blood soaked his fingers while she rummaged through his pockets. Caleb was glad he'd left his pocket watch at the cottage.

She hissed in frustration. "Thanks for nothing."

She delivered a hard kick to his gut before disappearing down the alley.

Caleb lay on the cold, wet ground, shivering as pain pulsed through his side. His eyes fluttered shut. He didn't have the strength to move.

A vision tore through his mind without warning.

He saw himself from above. He was sprawled on the ground, blood pooling beneath him. A tall figure staggered into the alley, his shoes splashing through the puddles. The man's face stayed hidden as he gripped a broken bottle in his hand.

He crept closer, the jagged edge raised. Before he could strike, the vision vanished.

Caleb's eyes shot open as wild panic ripped through him. His gaze snapped around the alley. It was empty, but it wouldn't stay that way.

He had to leave—*now*.

Gritting his teeth, he made himself move. He staggered upright, soaked to the bone. One hand clutched his wound while the other braced against the brick wall to keep him standing. A groan slipped from his throat, and his body screamed at him to stop, but he couldn't.

He stumbled forward, lightheaded with each step as blood soaked through his fingers. Olivia faded from his thoughts. All that mattered now was getting back to the cottage.

His gut twisted as he dragged himself down the alley and crossed the empty street. His legs felt heavy and uncooperative, but he forced them to keep moving. He didn't stop until the cottage came into view. Thankfully, he made it inside without running into anyone else.

The sight of the empty room hit harder than the wound. Olivia still wasn't home.

Clutching his side, Caleb stumbled to the closet and dug out the medical supplies. His hands shook as he cleaned the gash and pressed bandages into place, biting back a groan when fresh pain flared.

When it was done, he sank onto the sofa. The cushions dipped beneath his weight as he leaned back and closed his eyes, waiting for the medicine to dull the pain.

He was safe...for now.

***

"I never found Olivia."

Caleb leaned back into the barstool and crossed his arms. "After my wound healed, I searched everywhere. The city. The forest. Places I shouldn't have gone alone." He shook his head once. "She was gone."

Adeline stayed quiet, recognizing the familiar ache of loss.

"I kept searching for about a week. Then I realized I was on my own," he said, dragging a hand over his shaved head. "The diner didn't pay enough, so I quit. I started stealing instead." He paused. "After a few months of that, I decided to try to escape again. I didn't care what happened to me anymore."

Adeline leaned forward slightly. "Ralock stopped you?"

"Yeah. I figured he would," he said, his frown deepening. "I just didn't expect how badly."

Chapter Twenty-Five

The full moon was the only light guiding Caleb as he ran through the forest, his dreadlocks whipping against his neck. Branches lashed at his face and arms, stinging as he pushed past them.

The territory line wasn't marked, and everything looked the same in the dark. Still, something deep in his gut told him he was close.

His heart thundered in his ears as his breath came hard and fast. He'd already been running for over a mile, but it felt more like a marathon. His body was too thin now, his strength draining far faster than it should.

Swish!

An arrow sliced through the air beside his head, close enough that he felt it pass. Adrenaline surged, and Caleb pushed harder. He wasn't alone anymore.

Footsteps thundered behind him, closing the distance with every stride.

Too afraid to turn around, Caleb kept sprinting as his lungs burned. Every breath scraped his chest raw, but he kept going.

He veered into a zigzag, leaping over rocks and crashing through bushes as arrows hissed past him, slicing through branches where he'd been seconds before.

Slam!

Fire exploded across his upper back as an arrow drove into his right shoulder. The force of the impact sent him face-first into the dirt.

A broken sound tore from his throat as he clawed at the forest floor, dragging himself forward while heavy steps closed in behind him.

"We figured you'd try to leave again," the hunter taunted. Dressed in green leather armor, he slung his bow over his shoulder, then reached down and ripped the arrow from Caleb's back.

A scream ripped free as fiery pain blasted through him. His body jerked against the ground as warm blood soaked his shirt.

The hunter laughed. He seized Caleb by the arm and hauled him up, then drove a brutal punch into his face.

White light exploded behind Caleb's eyes. He sank back to the ground, the impact ringing through his skull. Cold earth pressed against his cheek as the forest blurred. "Jesse," he whispered, his voice breaking.

He hadn't called for help in a long time. He wasn't sure why he was calling now. They would never come for him.

"Still trying to summon your friends, I see."

The voice slithered through the darkness.

The hunter looming over Caleb straightened and turned. Footfalls approached, stopping just behind him.

Caleb pried his eyes open. The blood drained from his face when he saw the man standing there. His camouflaged features were nearly identical to the other hunter's, but the tip of his nose was gone.

There was no mistaking him.

Cutler.

Cutler fisted a hand in Caleb's dreadlocks and yanked his head up. He leaned in close, his breath warm against Caleb's ear. "You're Ralock's property, which means you can *never* leave."

He slammed Caleb's head back into the ground.

The impact stole what little air he had left. His body trembled as he wheezed against the earth pressing into his face. He wished it would just end.

It didn't.

Cutler drew a black dagger from his hip and drove the tip into Caleb's back.

Caleb screamed as the blade carved into his flesh, slow and deliberate. He thrashed against the ground as pain detonated through him, his cries echoing through the trees.

Cutler slowed when he reached the arrow wound in Caleb's shoulder. Then he pressed the blade in and pulled downward.

Another cry ripped from Caleb as his body convulsed.

"You should've learned your lesson the first time," Cutler said. He stood and wiped the bloody blade on his armored pants. He looked down at Caleb, his mouth curving into a thin, satisfied smile.

"What should we do with him?" the other hunter asked. "He won't last the night with those wounds."

"Leave him," Cutler said, sheathing his dagger.

The hunter faltered. "The master has strict rules about killing his followers without permission."

Cutler slapped him across the face. "I said leave him," he snarled. "Now go."

The hunter threw Caleb one last look before turning and disappearing into the trees. Cutler followed without another glance back.

The forest fell silent.

Caleb lay alone, his body shaking as darkness crept in and out. He closed his eyes, unsure whether he would open them again.

***

"Caleb," a firm voice said from the darkness. "Wake up."

Caleb opened his eyes. The forest stood unnaturally still, bathed in moonlight. He felt no pain. No weight in his body at all.

Am I dead?

Then he saw her.

Olivia stepped out from between the trees, dressed the same way she'd been the day she disappeared.

"Olivia." He rushed forward and wrapped his arms around her. "I've looked everywhere for you."

She pulled back slightly, just enough to meet his eyes. "Find the night-flowers," she said, urgency threading through her words. "They're purple and only bloom at night, growing along the vines of certain trees. You don't have much time. Eat them. They'll help you heal."

"Night-flowers?" he asked, his face scrunching. "Why do I need them?"

She pointed to his chest, and he glanced down. Blood spread across his shirt, blooming red without pain. Panic flickered as he looked back at her.

"Don't give up, Caleb." Olivia released him and stepped back.

He reached for her, but his fingers grasped empty air.

She was gone.

"Olivia!"

***

Caleb jolted awake, sucking in a mouthful of dirt as panic seized him. His face was still pressed to the forest floor.

Pain crashed over him all at once. His head throbbed violently as raw, burning agony flared across his back.

Olivia wasn't there. It was only a dream.

Whether it hurt more to lose her again or to feel his body failing him, he couldn't tell. All he knew was that blood still soaked the ground beneath him, and his strength was fading fast.

He didn't have much time left.

Shutting his eyes, Caleb shivered uncontrollably as the pain worsened, dragging his mind toward darkness. He waited for death to come as the dream drifted through him.

Night-flowers.

He'd never heard of them. He didn't know if they were real or just his mind grasping for something to save him.

With effort, he forced his heavy eyes open.

It took everything he had to lift his head. Moonlight filtered through the trees, revealing tangled greenery and towering trunks all around him. His vision wavered as he searched, fighting to stay conscious.

Something purple caught his eye.

A massive oak loomed beside him, its rough bark traced with a vine climbing upward. And woven through the green leaves were small indigo flowers, no bigger than a fingernail.

Night-flowers.

They were within reach. If only he could grab them.

It took him several moments to gather the strength to lift his arm. Fire licked through his back as he closed his fingers around a handful of them.

They were sticky in his trembling palm as if they were coated in sap. He brought them to his mouth, just like the dream had instructed him.

The petals were bitter at first, and Caleb nearly spat them out. Then they dissolved on his tongue, turning smooth and sweet like honey. The liquid slid down his throat, spreading warmth through his chest and limbs. The pain was still there, but he was no longer cold.

Slowly lowering his face back to the forest floor, Caleb shut his eyes as his battered body continued to throb. He didn't know what the small, purple flowers would do. They would either heal him, or he wouldn't wake when morning came.

At that point, he didn't care.

Chapter Twenty-Six

"I woke up the next day and realized those flowers had healed me," Caleb said, finally glancing over at Adeline. "The wounds on my back were sealed. Every one of them. I was still in pain, but I managed to make it to the cottage."

Adeline sat there silently, absorbing his story. She'd seen the scars on his back. The damage done by Cutler and other hunters. Her lips flattened. If she ever crossed paths with Cutler, she'd make him pay. "I'm sorry that happened to you."

Caleb tugged his sleeve lower, hiding his bruised knuckles. "I deserved it."

"No one deserves that, Caleb."

A flash of anger crossed his face as he balled his fist. "I was the one stupid enough to believe Ralock."

"Just because he tricked you doesn't mean you deserved to be tortured."

Caleb smashed his lips together, a muscle jumping in his jaw. He wanted to argue. Adeline could see it. Instead, he looked away. He sat there for a long while, staring out the window above the kitchen sink. A songbird darted past as sunshine spilled gently through the glass.

Adeline waited for him to continue, to finish what he'd started, but he never did. He just sat there, his mind somewhere else. She exhaled as she rose and cleared their dishes.

Caleb didn't glance over when she sat back down beside him. He clearly wasn't going to continue unless she pressed him.

"I want to know what happens next," Adeline said, pivoting to face him fully.

Caleb turned his head, his gaze drilling into her. It was blank and emotionless, coming from the one eye that still worked. "It's not too much for you?"

If she were honest, her emotions were a jumbled mess. She wasn't sure if she wanted to cry or punch something, but she wasn't going to tell him that.

"No," she said, holding his stare.

He turned away again, staring out the window. "I tried to escape again, but it didn't go well. I realized I wasn't getting out without a weapon." He paused briefly, folding his arms on the kitchen island. "Ralock's military were the only ones who had them. If I wanted to leave, I knew I'd have to steal one."

***

Wiping the moisture from his forehead, Caleb slipped into the narrow alleyway, grateful for the shade. The heat had been relentless, and so had his pursuit. For nearly two hours, he had followed the warrior through the crowded streets, never letting her drift too far from his sight.

Weeks. He had spent weeks tracking her movements, learning her habits, and memorizing her routes. She was by far the smallest warrior he'd seen. Though she was still deadly, she gave him the best chance of surviving if things went wrong.

The warrior staggered slightly as she climbed onto a weathered barrel outside the brick bar. Raising the chipped goblet, she took a long gulp before wiping her mouth with the back of her hand. She glared at the people passing along the cobblestone street, daring anyone to challenge her like she was itching to use the dagger strapped to her hip.

The city had no shortage of bars, but this one was the busiest. And the most dangerous.

She visited it often.

Caleb stayed in the shadows, watching. Though it would've been easy enough to slip inside and steal a drink of his own, he'd learned long ago to avoid places like this. Bars were a breeding ground for chaos, and this one was no exception.

He wouldn't make that mistake again.

So he waited.

Eventually, the bar door burst open, and two intoxicated men spilled out, laughing as they stumbled into the street. They collided with each other, barely staying upright, until one of them lurched sideways and knocked into the warrior perched atop the barrel.

Her goblet flew from her hand. The drink splashed down her dark armor and boots, igniting her temper in an instant.

She sprang to her feet, her blade already in hand. "You're going to pay for that," she snarled, pointing the knife at the drunken men.

The men jumped back as she swung, scrambling out of the blade's reach as a crowd formed around them. They spread out, circling the warrior with unsteady confidence. They were unarmed, but intoxication had stripped away caution. Grinning like fools, they closed in together.

Caleb stood rigid as the fight erupted, his pulse pounding with the roar of the crowd.

The warrior lunged. Her blade tore into one man's stomach, dropping him instantly. He hit the street hard, blood spilling across the stones.

The second man didn't retreat. Fury twisted his face as he charged, slamming into her and driving her to the ground. Her dagger skittered away across the cobblestones.

Now's my chance!

Keeping his eyes on the abandoned dagger near the barrel, Caleb slipped from the alley and edged closer to the fight. The crowd remained fixated on the chaos, oblivious to him or the weapon.

The warrior struggled beneath the man's weight, grappling desperately as he rained down blows without hesitation. Killing a warrior was a high crime, but in his drunken fury, the man clearly didn't care.

The fight was nearly over. If Caleb wanted the dagger, he had to move fast.

He darted forward and snatched the weapon from the ground while every eye stayed locked on the bloody struggle.

A sharp tingling sensation burst across Caleb's palm and crept up his arm as he ducked into an empty alley and tucked the dagger into the waistband of his shorts. He tugged his shirt down, making sure the weapon was fully concealed as he headed toward the cottage.

The chants from the fight echoed behind him as he made himself walk, not run. Drawing attention now would be a mistake.

He crossed several busy roads with his head down and his heart thumping. Every passing warrior made his muscles tense, and every civilian's glance felt like a second too long. But no one stopped him. No one even looked twice.

Once inside the cottage, he shut the door and pressed his back against the solid wood. He released a slow, shaky breath he hadn't realized he was holding.

I did it.

Caleb pushed his dreadlocks out of his face and drew the black blade from his waistband. As his fingers closed around the hilt, warmth bloomed in his palm and slithered up his veins.

Fear drained away as confidence took its place. He pressed his thumb to the sharp edge, knowing exactly how much damage a blade like this could inflict. He'd be unstoppable with it.

Olivia's warning surfaced in his mind. Dark Territory weapons were dangerous. And not only that. If he were caught with it, he wouldn't survive the punishment.

The thought faded as Caleb gave the blade a quick swing, satisfaction curling his lips. He was one step closer to leaving that awful place.

Chapter Twenty-Seven

THE POUNDING ON THE front door ripped Caleb from his sleep the next day.

His heart slammed against his ribs as he listened from his bedroom, every muscle locking in place. The sound came again, harder this time, sending a jolt of panic through him.

Who could it be? He never had visitors.

"Open the door!" a man called from outside.

Caleb swallowed hard. The iron bars across the front door offered a thin layer of protection, but they didn't ease the fear crawling up his spine.

The knocks continued.

Whoever it was, they weren't leaving.

Caleb crept out of bed and secured the dagger at his waist, tugging his shirt down to hide it. He crossed the cottage, every step measured. Cracking the door open, he peered outside.

A middle-aged man with a long, graying beard stood there, waiting. His thin frame was draped in a rough, makeshift tunic sewn from sackcloth, frayed and stained from years of wear. Red wolves gathered at his sides, staring at Caleb through the bars. Their stench was strong, their poor hygiene obvious, but that wasn't uncommon.

Caleb recognized the man, though he didn't know his name. He lived nearby in the woods with the wolves.

"What do you want?" Caleb asked, staying partially hidden behind the cracked door.

"I saw you yesterday," the stranger said.

A chill crept beneath Caleb's skin, and he fought the urge to glance at the dagger at his waist. "I don't know what you're talking about."

The man leaned closer to the bars, lowering his voice. "Yes, you do."

Goosebumps trailed down Caleb's arms as his hand gripped the door. He replayed the event in his mind, searching for where he'd messed up. He thought he'd been careful.

Apparently, not careful enough.

"I've been here many years," the man continued, giving one of the wolves a slow rub along its head. "And I want to go home."

"What does that have to do with me?"

"I need your help to escape. You...and that dagger."

Horror tightened his throat. He was caught, and there was no talking his way out of it. "What if I refuse?"

"I'll report you to the warriors," the man said plainly.

Caleb froze. If the man reported him, he was as good as dead. "Okay," he said, widening the door. "I'm listening."

The man smiled, yellow teeth flashing. "My name's Jack, and these are my wolves."

He swept an arm outward, motioning to the wild animals gathered around him.

They were everywhere—forty, maybe fifty of them—far more than Caleb had first assumed. Some lingered at the tree line, half-hidden in the woods.

"I'm Caleb," he said, keeping his eyes on the wolves.

"Nice to meet you, Caleb. Glad you've decided to help us escape."

Caleb cocked a brow. "Us? You mean the wolves?"

"Of course. I'm not leaving them."

"They don't have the mark," Caleb said. "Why don't they just walk out?"

"They can't leave either," Jack said, shrugging as a wolf brushed past his leg. "Any time they enter the red zone, the hunters kill them. That's why they stay with me."

"Why do you need me? You've got an entire pack to protect you."

"They aren't much help against the hunters," Jack said. "That's why I need someone with a weapon. A Dark Territory weapon."

Caleb eyed him suspiciously. "How do I know you won't just take the dagger from me?"

Jack lifted his right arm. Half of it was gone. "I'm useless with a sword now. That's why I need you."

Caleb didn't find that comforting. Still, he'd have a better chance at escaping with others. "Where do you plan on going?"

"Blistering Heights," Jack said, combing his fingers through his beard. "Ever heard of it?"

"No."

"It's far north, past the desert. You get me past the boundary line, and you're free to go."

For an instant, Caleb thought about going back to his world. Back to his old life. The thought didn't last. He was a different person now. He couldn't go back. Not now. Not ever. "I want to go with you."

Jack studied him. "Wouldn't you rather go home?"

"I have no home."

Jack eyed him for another second, then grinned. "The more, the merrier."

"When do we leave?"

Jack glanced toward the forest, where the wolves waited patiently. "I was thinking now. No point wasting any more time."

"Now?" Caleb repeated, unable to hide his shock.

Jack lifted a thick brow. "Is that a problem?"

"No. Give me ten minutes."

"I've got all the time in the world," Jack said. He stepped back from the door, and at once the wolves closed in around him.

Caleb shut the door, his mind reeling.

This was it. He was finally leaving for good.

***

Caleb splashed cold water on his face and stared at his reflection in the cracked mirror. Droplets dripped from his chin, tracing slow paths down his neck. He looked like a stranger, far from the healthy teen he'd once been.

His lips curled in disgust. He hated what the Dark Territory had turned him into.

A whiff of his own filth rose as he tried to scrub the dirt from his cheek with his hand. It didn't work. The grime had set into his skin now. He'd run out of soap months ago.

Using the hem of his old T-shirt, Caleb wiped his damp face and left the bathroom. His worn sneakers tapped softly against the hardwood as his grandfather's pocket watch knocked against his thigh.

He'd already eaten the last of his food and was ready to go.

The blazing sun was high in the sky when he opened the front door, the thick humidity rolling over him.

Jack stood motionless among the red wolves, their bodies fixed in place as if waiting for a command. "Ready?"

Caleb scanned the wolves through the barred door. "Will they attack me?"

"Not unless you attack me," Jack said, pushing a greasy strand of hair from his eye.

Caleb hesitated, anxiety surging. They could easily rip him apart. But what other choice did he have?

Stepping outside, he locked the door and secured the barred one. He threw the key into the woods. He wouldn't need it anymore. There was a spare hidden, in case their escape failed and he had to come back.

He refused to think about that.

Caleb kept his distance from the pack, his hand touching the dagger hidden under his shirt. His shoulders stayed tight as the wolves watched him with unsettling eyes. Everything in him wanted to bolt, but he couldn't.

"They won't hurt you," Jack said, stroking a wolf's matted fur. "I promise."

Caleb didn't respond. Promises meant nothing to him. He trusted no one, especially someone he'd just met. "How do you want to do this?" he asked, sweat collecting on his brow.

"We head north." Jack turned toward the forest and started walking. His pack followed.

Caleb cast one last glance at the cottage, then stepped after them.

He didn't look back.

Chapter Twenty-Eight

It didn't take long for Caleb's eyes to adjust to the darkness as they moved through the trees, the pack of wolves surrounding him and Jack like a shield. Moonlight sifted through the canopy above, offering just enough light to guide his steps.

They had been traveling all day. Even with the wolves at his sides and the dagger in his hand, Caleb couldn't shake the tension coiling in his chest. The fear of getting caught was still there, but it no longer ruled him. The blade grounded him, sharpening his thoughts and steadying his breathing as he pressed on.

He used the jagged blade to cut through low-hanging limbs and briars that scraped at his skin, tearing holes in his already worn clothes. He barely noticed. His focus stayed forward.

"We're in the red zone," Jack whispered, shoving a limb aside. "The border's close."

Caleb wasn't certain where they were, but his instincts told him Jack was right. His palms grew slick with anticipation as they continued. Tonight, he would leave and never come back.

Without warning, a rush of images flooded his mind, halting him mid-step. He watched from above as they raced through the woods, the hunters closing in behind them. Evergreen trees loomed ahead like a towering wall, freedom just beyond reach.

The wolves fell one by one. Hunters cut them down as Caleb and Jack ran, the forest erupting with chaos and blood. Then a single hunter stepped into Caleb's path, his long blade flashing in the moonlight.

Cutler.

"Kill him, Caleb!" Jack shouted.

Rage surged through him as he charged, hatred burning for the beast who had scarred his body. He swung—

But Cutler was faster. His blade pierced Caleb's chest, driving straight through him. He ripped it free with a laugh as Caleb collapsed, his blood soaking into the dirt.

Caleb gasped as he was thrown back into reality. He wheezed for air, his hand flying to his chest. No wound. No blood. He looked around wildly, only to find the wolves and Jack staring at him.

"Are you even listening to me?" Jack asked, grabbing his shoulder.

Caleb forced his breathing to slow, then shoved Jack away. "What did you say?"

"The evergreens mark the boundary line," Jack said, already moving. "We make it there, we're free."

Caleb nodded and followed as the wolves did the same. Cutler's taunting laugh still rang in his ears as they picked up speed.

Was he going to die? Or was it a warning?

There was no time to dwell on it.

Caleb ran.

His lungs burned as he pushed to keep pace with the pack, the wolves closing in around him and Jack as they surged through the forest, no longer trying to be quiet. Branches whipped at his face. Roots threatened to trip him. Every muscle begged him to stop, but he didn't listen.

An arrow screamed past him. It struck a wolf ahead with a sickening thud. The animal crumpled, its cry cut short.

"They're here!" Jack shouted.

Caleb and Jack ran on.

More arrows followed. They whistled through the trees, slamming into flesh and bark alike. Hunters were firing from all directions, hidden behind the trunks. Caleb ducked and weaved as adrenaline drowned out the pain, and rage narrowed his focus.

Hunters burst from the trees, blades raised. Wolves crashed into them, teeth snapping and claws striking as steel met them head-on. The forest erupted with snarls, screams, and the sound of bodies hitting the ground.

Some hunters broke past the wolves, ignoring them entirely as they headed straight for Caleb and Jack.

Caleb reacted without thinking, cutting in front of Jack as they sprinted. He slashed as he ran, his weapon cutting across exposed throats. Two hunters fell behind him, their bodies forgotten the moment they hit the ground.

Blood splattered his face. He didn't wipe it away.

The trees ahead began to thin.

Evergreens. They rose before him in a tight formation, thick branches braided together like a barricade guarding the boundary.

Freedom.

Ignoring his burning legs, Caleb vaulted over a fallen wolf and kept running with Jack close behind. The evergreens loomed closer as the stench of blood and death thickened the air.

I'm going to make it.

Time slowed as Cutler stepped into view, his sliced nose catching the moonlight. He didn't acknowledge the wolves spilling past him into the evergreens. His attention was solely on Caleb.

The long, jagged sword hung loose in his grip, already angled for the kill. Wolves rushed past him on either side, but Cutler didn't react.

He didn't want them. He wanted Caleb.

"Kill him, Caleb!" Jack shouted behind him.

Jack's words pounded in Caleb's head, reawakening the vision he'd just seen. Déjà vu slammed into him as his body kept running straight toward Cutler.

The dagger pulsed in his grip, feeding the fury that begged him to kill the monster who had scarred him for life.

It would be so easy. One lunge. One clean cut.

But he trusted the vision. He had already seen how it ended if he gave in.

Caleb veered sharply, sprinting at an angle.

"You'll never escape!" Cutler roared.

The evergreens rushed closer as Caleb ran, his sides cramping and lungs burning.

Cutler closed the distance and swung.

Caleb ducked just in time. Steel sliced past him as he plunged into the tangled branches. Pine needles raked across his face and arms, stinging his skin and snagging his clothes and hair. They were so thick he couldn't see where he was going, but he didn't stop.

He was free.

Cutler's roar reverberated behind him. "I'll find you—and kill you!"

Caleb kept pushing past the dense spruce trees, refusing to slow even as wolves ran alongside him. Cutler's furious shouts boomed behind him but grew fainter with every passing second.

Still, Caleb kept running.

Branches slapped his face as he shoved through them, the sharp cries of dying wolves ringing in his ears. He didn't let himself think about them. Distance was his only priority. He had to put as much of it as possible between himself and the Dark Territory.

He ran until his body gave out.

By the time he stumbled to a halt, the forest around him looked no different in any direction. Endless evergreens stretched in the dark. He didn't know where he was, only that he was far enough away...for now.

Caleb dropped the dagger and bent over, his hands braced on his knees as he fought for air. His legs trembled violently before giving out altogether, sending him to the forest floor. Pain flared through his chest and limbs as he lay there, gasping, staring up at the stars breaking through the trees.

A smile touched his lips.

He was finally free.

Wolves collapsed nearby, their breathing heavy as they sprawled along the dirt and pine needles. Shortly after, Jack stumbled out of the trees, just as winded, his remaining arm clutching his side as he flopped to the ground a short distance away.

They'd made it.

Caleb didn't know how many wolves survived. It was too dark to count, and he didn't care.

He was alive.

Chapter Twenty-Nine

Caleb woke the next morning with a stiff back and sore neck, still tucked beneath the cover of the evergreens. Every muscle protested as he slowly pushed himself upright, blinking against the pale light filtering through the branches.

The forest was quiet, and the air smelled of blood and pine as he surveyed the area. Sleeping wolves were scattered all around him, huddled in small groups. Jack was there too, sprawled on his back among them.

For a split second, Caleb thought he was dead.

Then Jack's chest rose.

Massaging the back of his aching neck, Caleb still couldn't quite believe he wasn't in the Dark Territory anymore. After so many failed attempts, he'd finally made it out.

But joy was far from reach.

The cobra tattoo coiled along his skin, a permanent reminder that he'd never truly be free. They would come for him. He only had a few days, a week at most, before they hunted him down.

His hand drifted to his pocket. The smooth curve of his grandfather's pocket watch pressed against his palm, and a rush of relief followed. He pulled it free and slowly flipped it open.

It was empty.

Panic spiked as he searched both pockets with fumbling fingers.

The note. Where was it?

Realization hit him.

He'd taken it out while cleaning the watch and never put it back.

Caleb pressed his fingers to his forehead, exhaling hard as frustration and grief twisted inside him. Grandpa's note was gone forever.

Jack stirred awake with a groan, rubbing his face as he sat up. The nearby wolves shifted and growled, disturbed by the movement. "We made it," he said, his voice rough with sleep.

"Yep." Caleb plucked a twig from his dreadlocks. "How many survived?"

Jack scanned the evergreens. "Hard to say. About a dozen or so with us. More will join."

Caleb gave a small nod and eased to his feet, careful not to startle the wolves sleeping nearby. Jack did the same, muttering under his breath as he found his footing.

Evergreens stretched in every direction, their long branches overlapping overhead, blocking out most of the sky. Pine needles carpeted the ground, and the trees crowded together, making it hard to tell one direction from another. There was no visible path, only an endless wall of green.

"Wake up," Jack said, shaking a wolf.

The wolf lifted its head with a low growl, its eyes flashing before recognition settled in. It rose slowly, favoring one leg, and immediately began licking at a blood-matted wound along its side.

Around them, the forest awoke. One by one, the other red wolves stirred. They stretched their stiff limbs, shaking the dirt from their coats as they lifted their noses to the air.

More shapes emerged from the evergreens, filtering in from all directions. At first, there were a few, then many more. Caleb counted them in silence, his chest tightening with each number. About thirty. Far more than he'd expected.

He still didn't trust them, but he was stuck with them now.

Caleb bent down and picked up his dagger. Warmth spread through his skin as he tucked it into his waistband.

"We'd better get moving," Jack said, brushing pine needles from his clothes.

Caleb nodded. "Lead the way."

They moved out in a loose line, the wolves slipping ahead and to the sides as if they already knew the way. The evergreens closed in around them, branches snagging at sleeves with each step.

Every stretch of forest looked the same as the last. Caleb couldn't tell if they were making progress or walking in circles. He focused on putting one foot in front of the other, letting Jack and the wolves guide him deeper into the trees.

They didn't stop often. When they did, it was brief.

They stumbled upon a shallow pond tucked between the roots of two massive pines. For a second, Caleb thought it was a mirage. He dropped to his knees and cupped his hands, drinking fast. The cold water washed over his dry tongue, cooling the rawness in his throat. The wolves drank beside him, the pond's surface barely rippling from their muzzles. No one spoke. Moments later, they were moving again, pushing through the evergreens without looking back.

Caleb found himself watching the wolves as they moved. They slipped through the trees without a sound, their eyes tracking everything. Their presence was unsettling, and Jack's presence among them didn't make sense.

"How come the wolves protect you?" Caleb asked.

"I saved one of them a long time ago," Jack said, knocking a branch out of his way. "They've stayed with me ever since."

Caleb glanced at the wolves again. Their loyalty to Jack was strange, but he left it alone.

They kept moving without stopping until the evergreens thinned and the forest stopped altogether. The shade vanished, replaced by hard sunlight and an open desert. Red earth stretched out ahead of them, cracked and bare, with jagged boulders rising toward the sky.

Cactuses and dry shrubs dotted the land among barren trees and rocks. It was a stark contrast to the dark green maze they'd left behind.

"Where are we?" Caleb asked, lifting a hand to shade his eyes.

"The Red-Rock Region."

Chapter Thirty

THE DAYS BLENDED TOGETHER as Caleb, Jack, and the wolves made their way through the treacherous desert. Heat pressed down on them from above and rose from the ground beneath their feet. Sand worked its way into their clothes and shoes, their skin raw from the sun and wind.

They ate and drank whatever they could find: dry roots, bitter plants, scraps of meat the wolves brought in, and the occasional mouthful of foul-tasting cactus water. They traveled early and late, resting only when they had no choice. Each mile deepened their exhaustion.

Caleb wasn't sure how much farther he could walk as he swiped sweat from his forehead. They hadn't been traveling long that evening, but the days of relentless heat had drained him.

"There's a spring close by," Jack said, his steps slowing.

Exhaustion screamed at Caleb to stop, to sink into the sand and stay there. Instead, he kept moving. The desert seemed endless, each mile blurring into the next. His legs shook beneath him, burning with every effort to lift them, but he couldn't quit. Not now.

Covered in dust from head to toe, he forced his weary legs forward, fixing his focus on the promise of water ahead.

They reached the watering hole as the sun dipped low in the sky. Clear water pooled between sunbaked stones and palm trees, their green branches bright against the surrounding desert. It looked like a tropical oasis had been placed there by mistake.

Caleb dropped beside the water and drank slowly, pacing himself. The coolness spread through him, easing the burn in his throat and chest. The relief was immediate. He closed his eyes for a brief second, savoring it. He'd forgotten how good water could taste.

"We can't stay long," Jack said, cupping water in his hand and drinking.

Caleb drank until he was satisfied and washed his face as best he could. He stepped away and sank beside a patch of prickly weeds, watching the red wolves crowd the pool. Their bodies pressed close as they drank.

He reached into his pocket and pulled out his pocket watch, rubbing his thumb over the worn gold. A heaviness settled over him. He still couldn't believe he'd left the note behind.

"Let's go." Jack straightened, water dripping from his graying beard.

"We just got here," Caleb said irritably.

"We have to make it to Blistering Heights before the hunters come for us."

Jack turned, and the wolves moved with him, peeling away from the water and falling in behind him.

Swearing to himself, Caleb stood and wiped the dust from his shorts. As he went to tuck the watch away, something bumped into him from behind, knocking him a step forward. His hand jerked open on instinct, but his attention was already elsewhere.

"Watch it!" Caleb snapped, catching his balance.

The wolf flashed its teeth. Caleb drew his dagger and pointed it at the animal.

"That's enough!" Jack said, his voice cutting through them.

Caleb kept the blade raised a second longer before lowering it.

The wolf growled once more before turning away and following Jack and the pack.

They continued beneath the stars, the desert cooling drastically the farther they went. Caleb hugged his arms around himself, trying to trap what little heat he could as the temperature dropped. Hunger gnawed at his sides as exhaustion dragged at his limbs, every step a sharp reminder of the blister rubbing raw against his foot. Still, they kept moving as the miles stretched on in silence.

The sun was beginning to rise by the time they finally stopped. They found shelter beneath an overhanging boulder and slept through the day, hiding from the worst of the heat.

Sleep came in waves for Caleb. The ground was hard and uneven, pressing into his aching body no matter how he shifted, and the desert was never quiet. Vultures circled overhead, and coyotes howled somewhere in the distance, their calls echoing through the rocky desert. Scorpions and tarantulas skittered through the rocks, along with snakes and rodents, but Caleb paid them no mind. Nothing came too close. The wolves made sure of that.

That was one good thing about having an entire hungry pack of wolves around.

The day wore on as they rested, heat rippling across the desert as the sun began its slow descent toward the horizon. The air reeked of decay and filth, baking in the blazing sun, but Caleb had grown used to it. He lay still in the shade of the boulder, watching shadows stretch across the sand as he waited for Jack to wake.

They should be moving soon.

Jack was several yards away, exactly where he'd collapsed. He hadn't moved.

Caleb's fingers slipped into his pocket out of habit. It was empty.

He sat up in a panic, searching the ground around him and patting his pockets again. The pocket watch wasn't there.

He searched frantically, sand scraping beneath his trembling hands as a hollow ache formed in his chest.

It was gone for good.

First the note, now the watch.

Caleb cursed, squeezing his eyes shut as pressure built behind them. He had nothing left of his grandfather. Nothing at all but faded memories.

A mournful whine sliced through the silence.

Caleb turned and saw a wolf crouched beside Jack, pawing at his stomach and nudging him with its nose. Its tail drooped as it whined again.

Caleb sprang to his feet, stumbling toward them. The wolf backed away, its ears pinned.

"Jack," Caleb said, nudging the man's bony shoulder.

Nothing.

He tried again, harder this time.

Jack didn't stir. He lay on his back, his eyes open but vacant as he stared at nothing. His mouth hung slack, and his chest was unnaturally still.

Caleb's breath hitched. "No."

He staggered back, raking his hands through his dreadlocks as fear and fury tangled inside him.

Jack was dead.

Caleb's gaze darted around the desert. He was alone, surrounded by a pack of wolves.

Panic clawed at his throat. How was he supposed to find Blistering Heights now? The only thing Jack had told him was that it was north.

The wolves shifted, their watchful eyes never leaving him. Would they see him as prey now? Or their new leader?

Caleb's hand slid to the hilt of his dagger, drawing it free from his waistband. Heat surged through his veins, replacing his fear with something else entirely. He felt strong. Invincible. Angry.

He forced himself to breathe. *Think, Caleb.*

He tipped his head back and squinted at the afternoon sun. Years of Boy Scouts kicked in, and it only took a moment for him to figure out where north was.

He'd stick with the plan and head to Blistering Heights. He didn't know if the wolves would follow, but he was moving on without Jack.

Chapter Thirty-One

Caleb moved north without looking back. He didn't need to look over his shoulder to know the wolves were there. They followed at a distance, their paws nearly silent against the hard ground. Dried blood crusted in their fur, and the sour stench of rot clung to them, but he no longer noticed.

He kept his dagger in hand and his pace steady as the late-day sun scorched the barren land, heat radiating off the sand in shimmering waves. There was nothing but open desert, yet danger could be anywhere. Boulders and rugged rock formations littered the ground, each one large enough to hide something…or someone.

He climbed over a rock—then froze.

The wolves did as well, lifting their noses to the wind.

Hooves. He could distinctly hear horses over the screech of vultures circling overhead.

Someone was coming.

Caleb darted behind a boulder, pressing his back against the stone as his pulse hammered. He leaned out just enough to peer around the edge in the direction of the sound.

Dust billowed in the distance, rolling across the desert floor as two horses emerged from the haze. The rhythmic thunder of hooves grew louder by the second.

Caleb immediately recognized the massive black stallion and the rider atop it.

Jesse.

Anger boiled in him as disgust curled his cracked lips.

The horses skidded to a sudden stop, hooves grinding into the sand as dust exploded around them. Caleb held still, barely breathing. When the haze finally thinned, his attention shifted to the second rider.

A girl.

She sat tall in the saddle, her posture calm in a way that immediately set Caleb on edge. He didn't recognize her, but that didn't matter. She was with Jesse. That was reason enough to hate her.

Caleb stiffened as the wolves fanned out from the rocks, low growls rolling from their throats as their eyes locked onto the newcomers. Missing limbs and infected wounds did nothing to dull their aggression. Their bodies tensed as they bared their teeth.

Caleb's mind reeled as anger and hurt twisted together. His grip tightened on the hilt of his dagger until his knuckles turned white.

An arrow struck without warning, slamming into a wolf's forehead and sending it crashing to the ground.

High-pitched howls ripped through the desert. The pack gnashed their teeth as they charged.

With Jesse and the girl distracted by the wolves, Caleb slipped through the rocks, unseen.

Chaos and death thundered through the desert, echoing off the stones as the fight raged. Caleb crept closer, keeping low, his breath shallow. Every wound he'd endured in the Dark Territory came rushing back. The loneliness. The pain. Being left behind.

Jesse would pay for abandoning him.

And the girl. Who was she? Jesse's girlfriend? A companion?

It didn't matter.

A wicked smile spread across Caleb's face as an idea took root. It was dark, intoxicating even. Killing her would destroy Jesse.

And that was exactly the point.

***

Adeline sat speechless, everything falling into place now. The Dark Territory. Olivia. The scars. The wolves.

"You know the rest," Caleb said, flicking her a quick glance.

She did. All too well. "You thought I was his girlfriend?"

"I didn't know who you were." He shrugged. "I just knew you were with him."

Adeline swallowed back the lump rising in her throat. She'd loved Jesse. Fiercely. Just not like that. "That's why you attacked me?"

"Yeah." He rubbed his jaw. "Seemed like a good idea at the time."

Adeline let out a small laugh, though a rush of emotion swelled in her chest. It had only been a few days prior, but it felt like a lifetime ago. She'd never forget their first encounter. "You followed us?"

"Yeah. You two weren't hard to track," he said. "Especially with that fire."

"But why?"

"I needed supplies. And a weapon, since someone broke mine."

Caleb gave her a crooked smile, and she returned it. She could still picture his solid black blade shattering like glass.

Adeline studied him quietly, replaying everything he had told her. Understanding settled in. What had started as a distraction had turned into something else entirely. She couldn't help but see him more clearly now. "Thanks for telling me your story."

Caleb dipped his head, releasing a breath that sounded like relief.

WHOOSH!

A sudden fire roared in the fireplace, flames leaping high and flaring across the hearth.

Adeline jolted as she stared into the blaze. She shot Caleb an alarmed look, making sure he was seeing the same thing. His bruised eye was wide and his posture tight as heat flooded the room.

Neither of them spoke.

The front door swung open, and Henry Snow stepped inside.

He looked worn down in a way she'd never seen before. His usually tidy clothes were rumpled and stained. So was his newsboy cap. He removed it slowly, revealing white hair dusted with dirt.

Adeline couldn't breathe as her heart thumped painfully fast. She wanted to run to him, to squeeze him, but she couldn't move.

Fear held her in place.

Henry looked at Adeline, his golden-brown eyes locking with hers. He smiled, and all the fear evaporated. "Hello, Addie."

Adeline leaped off the barstool, crossed the room in a few unsteady steps, and collapsed into his open arms. She clutched his small frame as her body shook, unmoved by his sweaty scent. Tears and snot soaked into his shirt as she sobbed against him, gripping him like she might never let go.

"I'm sorry, Henry," she cried.

"It's going to be all right, love," he whispered, rubbing her back.

"I killed Jesse," she said through her sobs.

Henry held her tighter. "It was an accident."

"I'll never forgive myself," she cried, clinging to him.

"Shh," he murmured, his accent gentle as his hand moved soothingly over her back. "Everything is going to be just fine."

As Henry continued to hold and console Adeline, his gaze shifted to Caleb, who was still planted on the barstool. Caleb didn't move, his body tensing.

"Welcome home, Caleb."

Caleb stayed glued to his seat, staring at his old friend. He didn't say a word.

Heavy footsteps pounded across the front porch.

Adeline pulled away from Henry and gasped as Godfrey stepped inside the cabin. A foul, metallic stench followed him in. Godfrey looked just as worn down and filthy as Henry. His bushy red hair was oily and tangled, and his clothes were soaked with sweat and blood.

But it wasn't his appearance that made Adeline's knees weaken.

It was the body in his arms.

Godfrey was carrying Jesse.

Adeline covered her mouth in horror, sobbing into her hand as more tears poured down her face. Jesse had been beaten, his body shredded nearly beyond recognition. The smell rolling off him was suffocating, and Adeline gagged. Godfrey gently laid his body on the dinner table, his limbs hanging loose and lifeless.

As Adeline continued to cry, Henry jumped into action, retrieving a bucket of water and a clean cloth from the kitchen before moving to Godfrey's side. Together, they carefully removed Jesse's torn shirt and began cleaning the blood from his skin.

Now that his chest was exposed, the damage was impossible to miss. A massive, blood-stained wound gaped in the center of his chest, surrounded by deep cuts that made it clear he'd been stabbed more than once.

Then she saw it—the place where her arrow had pierced him.

Adeline gasped for air as her heart ripped apart. Images of his death crashed through her mind, stealing her breath. The room tilted as she swayed.

Caleb launched from his seat and caught her just in time. His grip was tight but not rough as he held her up.

"Let's sit down," he said, guiding her to the couch.

They sat together, Adeline shaking as Caleb pulled a blanket around her shoulders. She clutched the fabric, her breath uneven as shaky sobs slipped free. He stayed close, offering his presence without a word.

Adeline glanced over, the blanket still wrapped tightly around her, as Henry and Godfrey worked over Jesse's body. They moved with careful focus, using the bucket of water and a cloth to wipe away the dried blood and filth clinging to his torn skin.

She tried not to look, but she couldn't stop herself. The sight made her stomach churn. Jesse had been beaten beyond anything she'd imagined possible. His skin was sliced and mangled, the damage so severe it was hard to believe this had once been the same man she'd spent most of her time with.

The water in the bucket turned dark almost immediately. Henry dumped it into the sink and returned with fresh water again and again.

Guilt clawed its way up Adeline's throat.

This is all my fault.

Jesse was dead because of her. Because of one mistake. One arrow she would never be able to take back.

She tore her eyes away from his body and looked to Henry and Godfrey instead. Their faces were calm and focused, as if they were preparing for surgery rather than tending to their son and friend. It would have been easier to bury Jesse as he was, yet they treated him with such care, as though restoring his dignity mattered, even now.

Her eyes drifted to Caleb. He sat beside her, silent and tense, his expression unreadable as he watched the same scene. Now that she knew his story, she wondered what was going through his mind. Did it hurt him to see Jesse like that? Was he still angry with Godfrey and Henry? Did he want to leave the cabin and never come back?

Whatever thoughts stirred in him seemed heavy enough to pin him in place.

The room felt thick with sorrow, pressing down on her until breathing became an effort. She'd known Jesse was dead. But seeing him there, the finality of it, made her heart ache even more.

"Are you going to bury him in the garden?" Caleb asked, barely audible.

Godfrey looked up. His electric blue eyes met Caleb's, not with anger, but with an unexpected warmth. "We aren't going to bury him, Caleb."

Adeline frowned and sat up, waiting for Godfrey to elaborate. He didn't. Instead, he turned back to Jesse, his features eerily calm as he stared down at his lifeless son. He didn't look angry. He didn't look sad. He didn't look upset at all.

It was strange. Adeline had expected rage, devastation...something. But Godfrey showed none of it. He simply studied Jesse's beaten face, brushing a long strand of hair away from his busted eye.

Then Godfrey leaned down, stopping only inches from Jesse's broken nose. "Wake up, Jesse," he whispered, then blew softly over him.

A thin stream of blue light poured out of Godfrey's mouth like smoke. It curled and twisted through the air, brushing over Jesse's face before slipping into his nostrils.

The sweet scent of jasmine filled the room, erasing the decaying odor in an instant. Jesse's chest shuddered, then began to rise and fall. Before Adeline could process what she was seeing, his open wounds sealed, and the bruises faded beneath his skin.

Adeline gasped and jumped to her feet. "What is happening?"

As soon as the words left her mouth, Jesse's eyes flew open. He dragged in a harsh, desperate breath like he'd been underwater. Just as quickly, his eyes shut again.

There was no denying it. Jesse was breathing on his own.

"This isn't possible." Adeline jammed her hands through her hair. "He was dead."

"He isn't anymore," Godfrey said as he brushed Jesse's hair back from his face. "It will take some time for him to fully recover, but he'll be as good as new before you know it."

Tears poured down Adeline's face as Godfrey's words sank in. She didn't know how to respond as he lifted Jesse from the table and carried him across the room. He moved with deliberate gentleness, yet Jesse still let out low, painful moans. Godfrey disappeared down the hall, Jesse's pained sounds fading with him.

Adeline was too stunned to move. So was Caleb. He sat frozen, his mouth hanging open. The fire crackled and popped, too loud in the sudden stillness, as her mind spun out of control.

What they had just witnessed was impossible. Jesse had been dead. She had watched him die. She had seen his fatal wounds.

And yet...he was alive.

Her hands trembled as the truth became clear. She needed answers.

Adeline finally stepped into the kitchen. Henry stood at the sink, washing his hands as if nothing extraordinary had happened.

"Henry." Adeline approached him, wrapping her arms around herself. "What just happened?"

"We brought Jesse back to life," Henry said simply as he dried his hands.

"But *how?*"

"My dear girl." Henry smiled gently and rested his aged hand against her cheek. "You of all people should know we can do anything."

Adeline had experienced strange and unexplainable things in that realm. Things that defied logic and reason. But she had never seen anything like this. Nothing that could steal someone from the grave. She'd known her friends had power, but this was an entirely new level.

"What about Regal?" she asked, her words shaky. "Did you save him too?"

"Yes," Henry said, his wrinkles deepening as he grinned. "He's recovering in the barn."

Adeline choked out a laugh as tears spilled over. She pressed her hand to her mouth, her heart swelling with gratitude and relief. Regal was alive too.

The heaviness in her chest eased. The tears kept coming, and there was no stopping them now.

Chapter Thirty-Two

Godfrey returned from the hallway not long after, his broad shoulders filling the doorway. He looked tired, but the familiar grin on his freckled face widened when his eyes found Adeline.

She rushed to him before she could stop herself, throwing her arms around his wide frame as her heart threatened to burst.

Godfrey wrapped her in a warm embrace, holding her close. Relief pooled in her stomach as she dug her fingers into his shirt, and for the first time since everything had gone wrong, she felt like she could actually breathe.

"I'm sorry," she whispered, the words breaking apart as she pressed her face into his chest.

"There's no need to apologize," Godfrey said, resting his chin atop her head.

"I killed your son."

"He isn't dead."

Adeline pulled back to look up at him, tears streaking down her face. "You're not mad at me?"

"Of course not." Godfrey lifted his hand and gently wiped away her tears. "All is well, Addie."

Adeline searched his crystal blue eyes and knew he meant it. There was no judgment or anger there, only the same love and kindness he had always shown her. He wasn't going to banish her from the cabin. He wasn't going to hate her forever.

The tight knot of fear that had been coiled inside her since Jesse's death unraveled instantly.

"We can talk more later," Godfrey said, giving her a reassuring smile. "But right now, I need to talk to Caleb."

Godfrey looked at Caleb, who was still seated by the fire. He hadn't moved or spoken, his face tight with nerves and anger as the firelight flickered across it.

"Can we talk on the porch?" Godfrey asked, motioning toward the front door.

Caleb swallowed, his Adam's apple bobbing. He didn't answer right away.

Finally, he stood and slowly headed for the door.

Godfrey and Henry followed him outside. They settled onto the porch, Godfrey and Henry taking the porch swing while Caleb crossed his arms and leaned against the railing.

Adeline lingered in the kitchen, resting her hip against the counter as she sipped the water she'd gotten from the fridge. Her eyes kept drifting back to the porch. She couldn't hear them, but she watched anyway.

Caleb was shouting, his arms cutting through the air. His shoulders were stiff as he paced, stopping abruptly before flaring up again. Even from inside, his anger was impossible to miss.

Henry and Godfrey remained calm, their postures relaxed. They didn't raise their voices or move from their seats. Instead, they spoke calmly as if his anger didn't faze them.

Back and forth they went, the tension rising and falling, until Caleb's anger finally fizzled out. His shoulders sagged, the fight draining out of him instantly. He covered his face with his hands and sobbed openly on the porch.

Adeline's heart pinched as she watched him break. Whatever they'd said had finally gotten through to him. She hoped, more than anything, that this was the beginning of mending what had been broken.

Godfrey rose from the swing and pulled Caleb into his arms, holding him as he wept.

Adeline looked away, choosing to give them some privacy. She wished she could hear what was being said. Maybe Godfrey or Henry would tell her later.

Adeline looked back at the crackling fire, the soft pop of the logs filling the silence. Her thoughts drifted to Jesse. Was he sleeping? Was he in pain?

She couldn't shake him from her mind. She had to see him.

Nerves fluttered inside her as she eased into his bedroom, careful not to make a sound. The lights were off, but the remaining sunlight spilled through the windows, illuminating the room well enough for her to see him clearly on the bed. One look at him stopped her cold. He was on his back, his breathing steady and his face relaxed as he slept.

For a split second, she almost fled, but her feet carried her forward.

Adeline moved to the edge of the bed and sat down, the mattress dipping beneath her weight. She tensed for a moment, then relaxed when Jesse didn't stir. He looked peaceful as his soft snores invaded the stillness.

A tightness grew in her chest as she watched him, half-expecting him to vanish if she blinked. She grabbed his hand, the warmth from his rough skin confirming he was really there.

She still couldn't believe it.

Excitement and fear twisted her insides. Part of her wanted to wake him and beg for his forgiveness, while another part was too ashamed to say a word. Godfrey and Henry weren't upset with her, but what if Jesse was? He was the one who'd been stabbed and beaten to death.

Adeline sat there for a while, holding his hand as she watched him sleep. The sun slipped lower, its warm glow stretching across the room before slowly fading. Yet, she couldn't bring herself to leave.

A gentle knock on the door made Adeline jump. She glanced over her shoulder, her pulse still racing when she saw Henry leaning against the doorframe. His white hair and clothes were still disheveled as he tucked his hands into the pockets of his trousers. "How is our friend doing?" he asked quietly.

"I think he's okay." Adeline turned her attention back to Jesse. "He's been sleeping the whole time."

Henry entered the room and sat down beside her. "He will get better."

Tears welled in her eyes. "Do you think he'll ever forgive me?"

"He already has, Addie."

She looked over at him. "How do you know that?"

"I just do," he replied, giving her shoulder a gentle squeeze. "He loves you dearly, and he already knows it was an accident."

"I hope you're right," she said, wiping the tear that escaped.

"I'm going to freshen up and then start dinner." Henry stood and offered a soft smile. "Let me know if you need anything."

"Thanks, Henry."

Henry left the room, shutting the door behind him. The last of the sunlight had faded, but Adeline didn't move as gratitude flooded through her. She hadn't lost Henry or Godfrey. The relief was overwhelming.

But what about Jesse?

She lifted a shaky hand to her forehead and released a slow breath. All the memories she'd shared with Jesse crowded her mind. She closed her eyes as more tears fell. She couldn't lose him. Not again.

Giving his hand a gentle squeeze, Adeline vowed she would do anything it took to win his forgiveness. Because losing him once had nearly destroyed her.

CHAPTER THIRTY-THREE

BY THE TIME ADELINE wandered into the kitchen, Henry was already there preparing dinner. He'd showered and changed into a fresh button-down that was already dusted with flour as he rolled out pizza dough on the island. Homemade sauce simmered on the stove. Adeline breathed in the comforting smell and smiled. She loved his cooking.

The fire was still crackling and popping as Adeline did a quick sweep of the room. Godfrey wasn't around. He was probably showering.

Through the window, she spotted Caleb still on the porch. He was seated on the swing, staring out into the darkness. She felt the pull to go to him, but she wasn't sure if she should. What if he wanted to be alone?

"He would love your company," Henry said, rolling the dough into a neat circle.

"Are you sure?"

"Yes." The lines around his eyes creased as he smiled. "Why don't you take him his favorite drink?"

"Which is?"

"Sweet tea. I just made a fresh batch."

Adeline picked at her nails as she stared out the window at Caleb. Although she now knew his story, she still didn't know him well.

Before she could talk herself out of it, she went to the fridge, poured a glass of sweet tea, and carried it out the front door.

Caleb glanced her way, the porch light revealing the bruises on his face. She couldn't tell if he was glad to see her or not.

"Can I join you?" she asked, holding up the glass. "I brought you a drink."

"If you want to," he said, his gaze returning to the yard.

Crickets chirped loudly as Adeline sat beside him. The swing swayed beneath them. "Here," she said, holding it out to him.

"Sweet tea," he said, cracking a tiny smile as he accepted it. "How'd you know?"

"Henry told me."

Caleb lifted the glass to his busted lip, wincing as he took a small sip. He took another quick sip, then relaxed into the swing. "I forgot how good this is," he said, cradling the tea in his lap.

Adeline smiled. "I'll have to try some later."

Silence stretched between them as they watched the lightning bugs flicker across the yard, their soft glow drifting beneath the stars. The swing creaked faintly as they rocked. The quiet wasn't awkward at all. Instead, it was comfortable, as if she'd known him for years.

She still couldn't believe she was sitting beside the same guy who'd tried to kill her a few days ago. So much had changed in such a short time.

"I bet it's weird seeing Henry and Godfrey again," she said.

Caleb shifted slightly, tightening his grip on the glass. "You have no idea."

The quiet settled in, and Adeline wished she could read his mind. What had they talked about? Why had he cried? Was everything all right between them now?

"I can tell they're glad you're here," she said finally.

Caleb took another sip of sweet tea, the ice clinking softly. He kept staring out into the yard.

Adeline waited, unsure if he'd heard her.

"They want me to stay here with them," he said.

"They do?" Adeline sat up. "Are you going to?"

"For now. I have nowhere else to go."

An unexpected flutter stirred in her chest. She couldn't explain it, but something in her was glad he wasn't leaving. "So...are things good with you guys now?"

Caleb gave a small shrug. "Better than they were."

Silence returned, thicker this time.

He stared out into the darkness for a while before speaking again. "I wouldn't be alive if it weren't for them."

"What do you mean?"

He swallowed hard, his shoulders tensing as if bracing himself. "Olivia."

Adeline's eyes went wide. "They know Olivia?"

"Yeah," he said, emotion catching his voice. "They…uh…asked her to take care of me."

Adeline's hand flew to her mouth as everything clicked into place. Henry, Godfrey, and Jesse were the reason Olivia had taken Caleb in. Why she had sheltered him, fed him, and protected him. All this time, they'd been helping Caleb without him ever knowing.

"Did they tell you what happened to her?" she asked, hesitant to bring it up.

He nodded as he hung his head. He sniffed, dragging his sleeve across his nose. "She died."

Adeline's heart sank. She'd had a feeling that was the case, but had hoped she was wrong.

Caleb cleared his throat as he quickly wiped at his eye. "She got caught smuggling weapons. When she wouldn't talk, Ralock killed her."

"I'm sorry, Caleb."

He stared down at the drink in his hands, rolling it slightly as the ice shifted inside. He shook his head once, as if he were still trying to make sense of it all. "I hated them the whole time I was there, and they were the ones who kept me alive."

"That doesn't surprise me," she said, almost in a whisper. "They aren't like most people."

"You've got that right."

Adeline fidgeted with her hands. "I thought for sure they'd hate me for what I did. I've never met anybody like them."

"Me neither."

The porch fell quiet again, broken only by the faint creak of wood beneath their weight. Adeline stared out into the darkness as the cool night brushed against her skin. Whatever Henry, Godfrey, and Jesse were, they had changed both her life and Caleb's in ways she was only beginning to understand.

Chapter Thirty-Four

THE SMELL OF FRESH pizza filled the cabin as Adeline sat on the couch with a plate in her hands. They didn't normally eat by the fire, but she was glad for it. Melted cheese stretched from the slice as she took her first bite. The burst of flavor made her take another. She shut her eyes, savoring the taste. She hadn't realized how hungry she was.

Beside her, Caleb ate slice after slice, hardly pausing between bites. Yet even as he did, his body stayed tense as if he couldn't fully relax. She couldn't tell if he was uncomfortable here or if he simply didn't know how to let his guard down anymore.

She hoped that in time he would learn to feel safe again.

The comfort of the cabin and the steady crackle of the fire wrapped around them as they ate. No one spoke much. They didn't need to. After everything they'd endured, the quiet felt right.

When the plates were finally cleared and the fire burned low, Adeline stared into the flames, her thoughts drifting back to the Dark Territory. It wasn't just what she had seen that haunted her, but also the details Caleb had revealed. How would he ever recover from that? And another question...

"How did you get Jesse?" she asked, looking between Godfrey and Henry. "That place was crawling with Ralock's military."

Godfrey folded his hands over his large stomach, his expression calm. "Ralock returned him to us."

Adeline frowned. "Returned him?"

"Yes."

She turned fully toward him. "You're telling me you just walked into the Dark Territory and took Jesse's body without a fight?"

"Yes." Godfrey nodded. "Ralock knew better than to refuse."

Adeline thought back to her first encounter with Ralock. He'd been afraid of Godfrey. She had seen it in his eyes. But why? Godfrey wasn't violent. He didn't even carry a weapon. "Why is he afraid of you?"

"Because he knows what I'm capable of," Godfrey said, the firelight flickering across his face. There was no arrogance in his voice, just certainty.

Adeline swallowed. Whatever he meant, she believed him. "Well," she said, rubbing her eyes, "I'm glad you were able to bring him back."

"So are we," Godfrey said.

The conversation faded into silence as more questions crowded Adeline's mind. There was one in particular that refused to leave. She hesitated, glancing at Caleb. Hopefully, he wouldn't mind her asking it.

"How was Ralock able to look like Caleb's grandfather?"

Caleb stiffened beside her, his fingers curling against the cushion. His eyes flicked to Godfrey.

"Ralock can alter his appearance," Godfrey said, directing his attention to Caleb. "He knew your grandfather. That's why he took his form. He knew you would trust it."

"Grandpa knew Ralock?" Caleb asked, disbelief edging his voice. "How?"

"He met Ralock in the forest before he found us," Godfrey explained. "Ralock showed him his territory and offered him gifts, hoping to win his loyalty. Fortunately, your grandfather refused the mark and found our cabin shortly after."

"Did Grandpa tell Ralock about me?"

"Yes," Godfrey said. "You were just a baby back then, but your grandfather couldn't help but sing your praises."

"That's how he knew my nickname," Caleb said, more to himself than anyone else. "But how did he know what I looked like?"

"He'd seen you come and go between your world and ours," Godfrey said. "It wasn't difficult for him to assume who you were."

Caleb scrubbed his hands over his shaved head. "He impersonated Grandpa for months. Why?"

"To trick you," Godfrey said. "Ralock gains power whenever someone takes the cobra mark. But someone from your world gives him far more. That's why he went to such lengths to deceive you."

Caleb stared back into the fire, saying nothing.

Adeline sat still, stunned by what she had just learned. She hadn't considered that Caleb's grandfather might have known Ralock. But it made sense. He had traveled to that realm for years. So had his ancestors. Had they crossed paths with Ralock too?

More questions stirred in her mind, leaving her head spinning. She wasn't sure she could handle any more tonight.

The fire crackled softly as shadows moved along the cabin walls. Adeline stifled a yawn. If she closed her eyes now, she wouldn't open them again. She pushed herself to her feet, her muscles protesting. "I'm going to bed."

"Goodnight, love," Henry said, offering her a soft smile.

"Sleep well," Godfrey added.

"Night," Caleb murmured, barely looking up.

She turned and walked down the dim hallway, the glow of the fire shrinking behind her. The cabin felt cooler with each step.

The floorboards creaked softly as their voices lowered behind her. She couldn't make out the words, only the hushed conversation just out of reach.

Part of her wanted to stop, to press herself against the wall and listen, but she kept moving.

She entered her room and shut the door behind her.

They had a lot to talk about.

She was sure of it.

Chapter Thirty-Five

Adeline woke before the sun had fully risen. Her muscles throbbed as she rolled onto her side, a dull ache pulsing through her skull. She brushed her fingertips over the tender spot on her forehead and closed her eyes.

She had thought for sure the lump would be gone by now.

Rolling out of bed, she dressed quickly and stepped into the hallway with one person on her mind.

Jesse.

She crept toward his bedroom, her steps careful on the wooden floor. The cabin was so quiet that even her breathing sounded loud.

Everyone must still be asleep.

At his door, she eased it open and slipped inside, shutting it softly behind her.

Soft morning light spilled through the window, gliding over the furniture Jesse had built with his own hands.

Jesse lay motionless, his chest rising and falling in a slow, steady rhythm. His long, wavy hair was tangled against the pillow, framing a face that looked far too peaceful for someone who had been dead the day before.

Adeline stepped closer, her heartbeat loud in her ears.

This should have been her.

Her fingers curled into her palms until her nails bit into her skin. The pressure in her chest tightened as the image of her arrow striking him flashed through her mind. She squeezed her eyes shut before the tears could fall.

She couldn't fall apart. Not now.

He was breathing. That was what mattered.

Another wave of remorse washed over her as she sank onto the mattress and stared at her friend.

Dirt and grime clung to his hair and thick beard, which had grown unruly along his jaw. The bruises and cuts that had covered his skin were gone.

He looked fine, but she knew he wasn't.

Beneath the blanket, his body still carried the truth of what had happened. She had watched the wounds close, but that didn't mean he was healed. Healing took time. And he would need a lot of it.

She prayed they wouldn't leave scars. Just thinking about it made her stomach clench.

Jesse stirred.

Adeline stiffened as his lashes fluttered and his green eyes slowly opened. When they found hers, her breath caught.

She didn't know what to do.

Should she cry? Laugh? Throw her arms around him?

Instead, she just stared, forgetting how to breathe.

Then Jesse smiled, and something inside her unraveled. "Hey, Addie."

"I'm so sorry," Adeline cried, collapsing against him without thinking.

He winced but wrapped a weary arm around her back anyway. "It's okay. I'm not upset with you."

"I shot you in the back," she said against his chest, her voice breaking.

"You didn't mean to."

She pulled back, swiping at her cheeks. "You're really not angry?"

He gave her the smallest shake of his head. "I promise."

His words eased something tight inside her. The guilt that had been gnawing at her loosened its grip. She had been so sure he would hate her. But he didn't.

"I thought I'd lost you," she whispered, brushing the last of her tears away.

Jesse's lips curved faintly as his eyes shut. "Not going to happen."

He drifted toward sleep again. His breathing slowed, steady and even.

"Are you in pain?" she asked. "I can see if Henry or Godfrey has something to help."

"It's nothing I can't handle." A faint grin tugged at his tired face. "But don't worry. We'll start training again soon."

"I don't doubt it." Adeline chuckled as she rose from the bed and stepped toward the door. "I'll let you rest."

"Addie," Jesse whispered.

"Yeah?" She paused at the door and turned.

"Thanks for getting Caleb here safely."

"You're welcome," she replied with a small smile. "And you were right. He's not that bad."

"Told you."

Grinning, Adeline opened the door. "I'll check on you later."

"Sounds good."

Adeline stepped out of the bedroom and eased the door shut behind her. She didn't move right away.

Jesse wasn't mad at her.

The thought sent a rush of relief through her, so strong it nearly made her laugh. She hadn't lost him.

The rich scent of fresh-brewed coffee drifted through the hallway. Someone was already awake.

She moved toward the front of the cabin, her steps lighter than they had been only moments before.

Godfrey and Caleb sat at the large island when Adeline walked into the open area. Godfrey was mid-story, clearly enjoying himself, while Caleb leaned forward on his elbows, his coffee cradled between his hands. He smiled at something Godfrey said, though tension lingered in his shoulders.

"Good morning, Addie," Godfrey called, turning with a grand smile. "Come join us."

Caleb gave her a brief glance before dropping his gaze back to his mug. His face was black and blue, one eye still swollen shut. She wondered how long it would take for him to heal.

"Morning," she said, moving toward the coffee pot.

Adeline didn't usually drink coffee, but she decided to give it another try. The one Jesse had made for her in the desert tasted like melted chocolate. She wanted that again. Maybe she could make it the same way.

She reached for a mug and poured herself a cup. Steam curled from the surface as she dumped in a heavy pour of vanilla creamer and more than a few scoops of sugar. After blowing on it, she took a careful sip.

"Not bad," she said, her eyebrows lifting.

It didn't taste like the one Jesse had made, but that was all right.

Godfrey chuckled. "Since when do you drink coffee?"

"Since today." Adeline grinned as she stepped up to the island across from them. Resting her elbows on the cool surface, she took another sip, letting the sweetness linger on her tongue. "I talked to Jesse."

"And?" Godfrey asked, lifting his mug.

"He's not mad at me."

"Of course not." Godfrey broke into a smile. "I'm glad you two spoke."

"Me too," she said, warmth settling in her chest.

Caleb hadn't said a word since she joined them. She glanced at him, but his focus never left the coffee in his hands. His face gave nothing away. Was he just tired? Or simply worn down from everything they'd survived?

She shifted her weight, and her ribs flared in protest. It was nothing compared to what he must have been feeling. She was sure of it. Just looking at him made her want to look away.

She wished she could do something. Anything.

Then an idea came to her.

If Godfrey could heal Jesse... he could heal Caleb too.

"Godfrey," she began. "You healed Jesse yesterday."

"Yes."

"Could you...do the same for Caleb?"

Caleb cut her a sharp look. His hands trembled, but his expression hardened. Something flickered in his good eye, but she couldn't read it.

So, she forced herself to focus on Godfrey instead.

Godfrey leaned back into his seat, amusement dancing in his eyes. He turned toward Caleb, his round stomach pressing against his pajama shirt. "What do you think, Caleb?"

Adeline held her breath.

Caleb shifted on the barstool, his shoulders stiffening. Despite the bruising along his face, a faint color crept into his cheeks. He kept his attention on the mug in front of him. "I...uh...don't know."

"Do you want to be well?" Godfrey asked, his tone turning serious.

Caleb swallowed, his grip tightening around the mug. He finally nodded.

Godfrey's face softened as he reached out, resting his large hand on Caleb's thin shoulder.

Caleb flinched, his body tensing as if he expected to be hit. Then he stilled.

"It won't hurt," Godfrey said gently.

Although his words were kind, Caleb trembled beneath his hand.

Caleb sucked in a sharp breath as a soft light pulsed beneath Godfrey's palm. The dark bruising along his cheeks faded, deep purple softening to yellow before disappearing entirely. His split lip sealed. The swelling around his eyes receded until both were clear and open.

Within seconds, his skin was smooth and unbroken.

Adeline blinked.

Caleb's hand shot to his face, his breathing heavy as his fingers traced the place where the bruises had been. Shock flickered across his features as he pressed against the skin that had been broken moments ago. He looked at Adeline, his golden-green eyes wide and startled.

Adeline nearly gasped. Without the bruises and swelling, he looked completely different. He was more striking than she'd expected.

"Whoa," Adeline breathed before she could stop herself.

Then he smiled.

Adeline froze.

The missing tooth was back. His teeth were straight and clean like they'd never been stained and damaged.

"Your tooth," she said, pointing toward his mouth.

Caleb touched his teeth, disbelief flashing across his face before a shaky laugh escaped him. He looked to Godfrey, who watched him with quiet satisfaction. "You fixed my teeth too."

"I sure did," Godfrey said, lowering his hand. "I figured you'd want your old smile back."

"Thank you," Caleb whispered.

Adeline couldn't move as she looked Caleb over. Old scars still lined his biceps, disappearing beneath the fabric of his T-shirt. She was sure the ones on his back were still there too, but everything else had healed.

Suddenly, Adeline's body turned scorching hot. Heat spread through her tight, aching muscles, kneading away the pain until nothing remained. Even her headache vanished in an instant.

"The bruises are gone from your face too," Caleb said, his jaw dropping.

Adeline lifted a hand to her cheek, her breath catching as her fingers traced skin that should have been bruised and swollen.

"Couldn't leave you out." Godfrey winked.

"Thank you, Godfrey," she said, a smile breaking across her face. "I feel...amazing."

The aches and pains from her last adventure were completely gone. She couldn't remember the last time she'd felt that good.

"I'm going to change," Godfrey said, rising from his seat. "And then I want to show you two something in the garden."

"What is it?" Adeline asked, her interest piqued.

"It's a surprise." He placed his empty mug in the sink before heading toward the hallway. "Be back soon."

Adeline watched him leave, her thoughts racing.

What could he possibly want to show us?

She felt Caleb's eyes on her and flicked him a quick glance. Her stomach did a somersault.

He was slowly looking her over like he was seeing her for the first time.

But when she caught him, he looked away quickly.

"Sorry," he said, ducking his head.

Heat rushed to her cheeks, but she tried to act casual. "It's okay. I think I'm just as shocked as you."

Caleb looked back at her, confusion clouding his features. "How did he heal us?"

Adeline shrugged. "I don't know. But I'm glad he did."

He dipped his chin in agreement and lifted a hand to his face again, as if making sure it hadn't changed back.

Adeline watched him quietly, still amazed by how different he looked without the bruises. It was hard to believe he had looked so beaten just minutes earlier.

Footsteps echoed down the hallway, and Godfrey reappeared wearing a tie-dyed shirt and loose shorts. A wide-brimmed straw hat sat snugly on his head, his red hair spilling out from beneath it. "Ready?" he asked, tipping the brim slightly.

Adeline exchanged a quick glance with Caleb before looking back at Godfrey. "Yep."

She had no idea what he was about to show them, but something in his smile told her it wouldn't just be a stroll through the garden.

Chapter Thirty-Six

THE MID-MORNING AIR WAS warm, a gentle breeze stirring the flowers around them like it was the middle of spring. Clouds drifted overhead, casting shifting shadows along the cobblestone paths while they wandered through the garden. The sweet scent of blooms lingered in the air as birds darted by.

It was a perfect day to explore.

Adeline walked between Caleb and Godfrey, soaking in the sunshine. A faint smile tugged at her lips as she breathed in the soft breeze lifting her long waves. It felt good to be outside.

Godfrey inhaled deeply, his jolly smile never fading as he took in the view, his flip-flops slapping lightly against the stones. Even Caleb seemed at ease. His usual stiffness gave way as he walked, his eyes drifting to the marble fountain where sunlight danced across the water.

Adeline slowed slightly as a thought resurfaced. The same one that had been bothering her ever since she learned Caleb was from Black Mountain. Time in her world always froze when she stepped through the portal and resumed the moment she returned. But Caleb had already been living here long before she arrived.

If time had paused for him when he came, how was she with him now?

"Godfrey," she said, glancing at him. "If time stops when we step through the portal, how am I here with Caleb? Wouldn't time have stopped in Black Mountain when he came here and got stuck?"

"It did stop," Godfrey said.

"It couldn't have."

"It did."

Adeline halted and put her hands on her hips. "You're not making any sense."

"When you go back, time will continue for you just like it always has... and the same will happen for Caleb," Godfrey said. "His life will pick up exactly where he left it."

Adeline turned to Caleb. "When did you last enter the portal?"

Caleb looked off to the side and scratched his head. "I'm pretty sure it was December."

"December?"

"Yeah." Caleb nodded. "I had just gotten Molly a Christmas present."

Adeline frowned. "But I came here in October." She looked back at him. "What year was it?"

Caleb told her.

Adeline's stomach dropped. It was the same year.

But he was two months ahead of her.

That meant Caleb was still living his normal life in Black Mountain when she'd last stepped through the gated forest. He wouldn't enter that realm and become trapped for another two months.

She looked at Godfrey, confused. "How is Caleb two months ahead of me?"

Godfrey smiled. "It will make sense when you go back and see it for yourself."

Adeline fell quiet as they continued walking. Her mind churned as she tried to piece it together. October. December. The same year. It made no sense. The more she thought about it, the more tangled the puzzle became.

She exhaled slowly and forced herself to move on, though the questions still remained. One glance at Caleb told her he was just as confused as she was. But he didn't say anything as he walked beside her.

The path eventually gave way to a stretch of freshly cut grass, bordered by towering trees draped in wisteria vines. Clusters of purple blossoms hung like grapes from the branches, forming a natural arch above the trail. Yellow forsythia bushes lined the ground beneath them, their color striking against the green.

Adeline slowed, taking it all in. She'd never been here before. It wasn't surprising, considering the sheer size of the garden.

Farther along, lupine flowers rose on either side of the path. Blue, magenta, red, and white blooms mingled with the other flowers, layering the garden with color.

At the end of the trail, they stopped. A wall of Eastern hemlock trees stood tall before them. Their dense branches formed a barrier. The dark greenery looked out of place among the bright flowers, and Adeline couldn't help but wonder why Godfrey had brought them there.

"Follow me."

Godfrey waved them forward. He stepped into the thick branches, parting them with his large frame until he disappeared from view.

Adeline and Caleb shared a quick look before following. Adeline went first, the branches brushing against her skin and catching in her hair as she forced her way through. She stumbled forward and froze, stunned by the view.

Caleb broke through a second later and stopped beside her.

They were in a hidden clearing. An oval stretch of freshly mowed grass was surrounded by the same trees and flowering shrubs that had lined the previous path. Wisteria and forsythia intertwined with towering Eastern hemlocks, forming a natural wall around the entire space, while vibrant lupine flowers added bursts of color throughout.

Two stone cottages stood inside the clearing, built from large rocks of varying shapes and sizes. One rested along the far-left edge, while the other stood on the opposite side.

Though similar in style, the cottages were slightly different in design. The one on the left formed an L shape, and the other was square with a steep triangular roof. Flowerbeds surrounded both homes, and a large stone fountain sat between them, encircled by benches and even more blossoms.

"Who lives here?" Adeline asked, shading her eyes from the sun.

"No one," Godfrey said, stepping toward the cottages.

Adeline tilted her head as he crossed the grass toward the one on the left. She and Caleb exchanged a glance before following him.

Built entirely of stone, it sat tucked against the trees, wisteria climbing along its sides. It was beautiful—too beautiful to be empty.

Godfrey walked straight to the front door and turned the knob before stepping inside. Adeline and Caleb followed close behind.

Sunlight poured through the open doorway and tall windows, spilling across the hardwood floors of the furnished living room. The stone walls matched the exterior of the cottage, and a fireplace immediately caught Adeline's attention. A thick slab of rock stretched across the mantel, and neatly stacked firewood sat beside the hearth, ready to be used.

The living space was modest, furnished with only a comfortable sofa and a recliner, yet it felt warm and inviting, the kind of place meant for cozy evenings beside the fire.

Taking a few steps to the left, Adeline entered a kitchen nearly the same size as the living room. A small square table sat against the wall, four chairs tucked neatly beneath it. Granite countertops wrapped the room beneath tall cabinets that reached the ceiling. The appliances were new, and a deep sink sat beneath a window that overlooked the lush garden outside.

"This place is amazing." Adeline turned slowly, taking in the cottage.

It didn't take long to explore. There was only one bedroom and a full bath, but the space was thoughtfully arranged and filled with everything needed to feel like home.

She paused in the living room, letting her gaze travel over the stone walls and warm furnishings. Something about the cottage felt peaceful, like the cabin.

"I love this place," she said, running her fingers along the arm of the couch.

Godfrey grinned. "I knew you would."

Adeline glanced around once more. "Why'd you bring us here?"

"Because I want to give it to you."

"What?" Her mouth fell open.

Godfrey reached into his pocket and pulled out a simple key. He placed it gently in her hand. "This place is now yours."

Adeline looked down at the key in her palm, her fingers trembling as she turned it over. She tried to steady her thoughts, but none of it made sense. She was only seventeen. Far too young in her world to own a home. Why would he do this?

"You're...giving this to me?"

"I am." Godfrey nodded. "And the other cottage will be Caleb's."

"Wait, what?" Caleb stared at him, his brows knitting together.

"You heard me." Godfrey drew another key from his pocket and extended it toward Caleb. When Caleb didn't take it, Godfrey placed it in his hand and gave it a firm squeeze. "It's yours."

"You can't be serious," Caleb said, staring at the key.

"I assure you, I am," Godfrey replied, happiness in his voice. "You'll always be welcome at our cabin whenever you like, but now you have the choice to stay in your own homes as well."

Adeline nearly burst with joy. "Thank you, Godfrey!" She threw her arms around him, barely managing to reach around his round middle.

Godfrey released a deep laugh and hugged her back with equal enthusiasm.

Caleb didn't move, his eyes glued to the key. "I don't deserve a house, Godfrey." He extended the key back toward him. "You should give it to someone else."

Godfrey didn't take it. "No one deserves it, Caleb. But I want to give it to you."

"Why?"

Godfrey's face softened. "Because I love you."

Caleb jumped as though the words had struck him. His jaw flexed, and he glanced away, blinking more than usual. For a moment, he didn't speak. When he finally looked at Godfrey, his eyes shimmered as though tears threatened to fall.

Godfrey patted him on the back. "Let's go check out your cottage."

Caleb used the crook of his arm to wipe his face before following Godfrey outside.

Adeline tagged along as Godfrey led Caleb back into the sunshine. The fountain trickled beside them, its steady rhythm carrying through the clearing as they crossed the grass toward the second cottage. Like hers, it was built of stone with wisteria climbing along the roof and spilling down the sides. The purple blossoms swayed gently in the breeze, their pleasant scent drifting through the warm air.

Caleb's hand shook as he stepped up to the front door and gripped the doorknob. It turned without resistance. He waited only a second before pushing the door open and stepping inside.

Adeline trailed close behind. The space opened into a similar layout, though the darker palette gave it a richer tone. A leather sectional faced the fireplace, and the kitchen's dark wood and brass accents added warmth. An oak dining table stood nearby, sturdy and built to last.

A slow smile spread across Adeline's face as she turned in a circle, taking it all in. "Wow! This place is amazing."

Caleb stood stiffly near the doorway. He shifted his weight from one foot to the other, his gaze moving over the room but never settling.

"What do you think, Caleb?" Godfrey asked, tucking his hands into his pockets.

"It's really nice. Are you sure you want to give it to me?"

"Positive," Godfrey reassured him. "Come on. I'll show you the rest of the house."

Adeline followed as Caleb moved through the cottage, lingering in each room. He ran his hand along the doorframes, stopped at the windows, and took in every detail without saying much. For once, he didn't look tense.

When they stepped onto the back porch, he paused. A pair of rocking chairs faced the woods, and a firepit stood ready to be lit. Something close to peace crossed his face.

"Now that you have both seen your new homes, here are a few helpful tips," Godfrey said as a cardinal darted past them. "These cottages have the same benefits as the cabin—unlimited clothing in the bedroom dressers and an endless supply of food and drink in your kitchens."

Adeline nearly squealed with excitement. Somehow, it just kept getting better.

"You both know the drill. If you think it, it will appear," he added, tapping his temple.

Adeline let out a breathless laugh. "This is awesome! I can't believe you gave us a house."

"Another thing." Godfrey held up a thick finger. "Ralock and his military sometimes roam through the garden, but they do not know about this hidden area."

All the color drained from Caleb's face. "What?"

"I don't want you to be afraid, Caleb," Godfrey said gently, "but you need to understand that you may run into them someday."

"I can't stay here." Caleb stepped back. "Ralock will find me."

"He can no longer track you," Godfrey reminded him. "He has no idea where you are. You'll be safe here."

"But what if he finds this place?" he asked, running his hands over his shaved head. "He'll send his hunters to capture me. I can't go back there."

"I know you've been through a lot, but you can't spend your whole life worrying about Ralock," Godfrey said, compassion softening his features. "And besides, you have Adeline as a neighbor."

"That's right." Adeline bumped his arm with a playful nudge. "I won't let anything happen to you."

Caleb's eyes were still clouded with worry, but his breathing slowed as he looked out at the beautiful view beyond the porch. Butterflies drifted lazily from one flowerbed to the next as sunlight filtered through the soft clouds. It was perfection, as if the garden itself had come alive just to welcome them. But Caleb didn't seem to see any of it.

His hand drifted to his forearm, his fingers brushing the place where the cobra tattoo had once been. He shut his eyes, as though trying to silence something only he could hear.

She understood now. Just because he was out of the Dark Territory didn't mean it was out of him. Its abuse and cruelty still clung to him, shaping the way he saw the world. Escaping it had only been the first step.

Healing from it would take time.

"I promise," Adeline said, breaking the silence.

Caleb hesitated before turning. His tall, thin frame cast a shadow over her as his golden-green eyes searched hers.

"You're not alone anymore." She touched his arm.

He flinched at first, a reflex he couldn't quite hide, and his gaze dropped to her hand like it didn't belong there.

But he didn't move away.

Slowly, he met her eyes again. The undeniable fear was still there. But this time, it was joined by something stronger.

Trust.

Something passed between them—unspoken, but understood—as he gave her a small nod.

Adeline didn't say anything else. She didn't need to. The quiet smile she gave him was enough.

She wasn't sure what the future held, but whatever came next, she would face it with her newest friend by her side.

THANK YOU FOR READING!

If you enjoyed this story, please consider leaving a quick review. Whether it's on Amazon, Goodreads, or wherever you picked up this book, your honest review makes a big difference. It doesn't have to be long—just a few words can help other readers discover this book. Thank you for being a part of this adventure. I can't wait to share more with you soon! If you'd like to be the first to hear about new releases and special offers, visit www.elizabethmowery.com to sign up for my newsletter.

Acknowledgements

First off, I want to give a huge thank you to God. Words cannot express how thankful I am for Your guidance. You are the foundation of every idea, every word, and every ounce of perseverance it took to complete this book. This story would not exist without You.

To my husband, Adam. Thank you for standing beside me through every step of this journey. You've supported me through the highs, the lows, and everything in between. I'm so grateful for you.

To my family, friends, and editors—thank you for your support, honesty, and the role you've played in shaping this book. This story is stronger because of each of you.

And finally, to you, dear reader. I cannot thank you enough for your continued support. I hope Caleb's story pulled you in and left you wanting more, because this adventure is far from over.

ABOUT THE AUTHOR

Elizabeth Mowery is an avid writer who has a passion for creating exciting stories that capture the imagination of her readers. She lives in the foothills of North Carolina, where she loves spending time with her family and friends. When she isn't writing, she can be found enjoying the simple pleasures in life—a hot cup of coffee, the fresh air of the outdoors, and a good book. Connect with her at www.elizabethmowery.com

9 798990 015159